The Fetti Girls 3

Lock Down Publications and Ca$h
Presents
The Fetti Girls 3
A Novel by *Destiny Skai*

The Fetti Girls 3

Lock Down Publications
P.O. Box 1482
Pine Lake, Ga 30072-1482

Copyright 2017 by The Fetti Girls 3 Destiny Skai

First Edition November 2017
Printed in the United States of America

Lock Down Publications
Like our page on Facebook: Lock Down Publications
@
www.facebook.com/lockdownpublications.ldp
Cover design and layout by: **Dynasty Cover Me**
Book interior design by: **Shawn Walker**
Edited by: **Lauren Burton**

Destiny Skai

Stay Connected with Us!

Text **LOCKDOWN** to 22828 to stay up-to-date with new releases, sneak peaks, contests and more…

Thank you!

Submission Guideline.

Submit the first three chapters of your completed manuscript to ldpsubmissions@gmail.com, subject line: Your book's title. The manuscript must be in a .doc file and sent as an attachment. Document should be in Times New Roman, double spaced and in size 12 font. Also, provide your synopsis and full contact information. If sending multiple submissions, they must each be in a separate email.

Have a story but no way to send it electronically? You can still submit to LDP/Ca$h Presents. Send in the first three chapters, written or typed, of your completed manuscript to:

LDP: Submissions Dept
Po Box 1482
Pine Lake, Ga 30072

DO NOT send original manuscript. Must be a duplicate.

Provide your synopsis and a cover letter containing your full contact information.

Thanks for considering LDP and Ca$h Presents.

Destiny Skai

Prologue

Barbee

After having a 30-minute meeting with the staff, we were ready to open the doors for business. Every supporter outside the door was let in, one-by-one. The DJ was on the ones and twos, spinning the latest Rick Ross joint, and the waitresses were walking around taking drink orders. I had to say I was impressed with the crowd standing before me. Mercedes and I sat back and waited for the doors to close before making an announcement.

Standing by the DJ booth, he passed me the mic and cut the music.

"Hello, everyone. I just want to say thank you for coming out to Chyna's Dolls. We greatly appreciate it. On your way in you were given a ticket, and that is for a free drink of your choice. A lot if you know me, and some of you don't. Originally, there were 4 of us who started this business, and now it's only the two of us because the others were taken too soon, which makes tonight bittersweet."

Thinking back to the day we thought of this made me choke up and freeze, losing my words. I was still in disbelief. Mercedes saw I was struggling and took the mic.

"Sorry, it's still hard for us because it's so fresh, but we want everyone to have a good time and turn the fuck up. Let's get lit in this bitch," she shouted.

Mercedes passed the mic back to the DJ and grabbed me by the hand. "Hey, we agreed there would be no tears shed tonight. We are going to mingle and have a little fun. After it's over, we'll have us a drink on the way home until we pass out."

"Okay. I can be so sensitive." I managed to chuckle a little bit.

"Only when you love someone," she laughed. "Let's go have some fun shit."

I was game for that, so I followed as she led the way.

For the next hour I mingled amongst the crowd, stopping to talk to the people I knew from the hood. Amon was also in the building.

"This shit lit, cuz." Amon hugged my neck. "I'm proud of you."

"Thanks, cuz. I appreciate that."

"Corey told me to tell you 'congratulations.'"

"Yeah, he could've called me and told me on his own. It's cool, though."

"This was hard for him to do, but he had to in order to get his self together. Us men," he patted his chest, "we love hard. And when we get hurt, it's like the end of the world. It may seem selfish, but it is what it is."

"Yeah, I see that." I frowned. What he was saying may have made sense to men, but it was crushing a bitch's heart.

Love should be stronger than pride.

Just when I was about to verbalize that thought to Amon, I saw his eyes widen with surprise, and he was staring over my shoulder.

Oh my god! My heart skipped several beats. I didn't have to turn around to know who he was staring at. It had to be my boo. I just knew there was no way Corey would miss my grand opening, especially when he knew what I went through to make this happen. Him surprising me felt so romantic. This was going to be a perfect night after all.

Smiling, I slowly turned around to greet my king with a hug and kiss, but the person I encountered was not him!

What the fuck?

My arms froze in midair. A tall black man wearing all black with a shiny badge around his neck stared at me with contempt.

My arms fell to my sides.

I cleared my throat. "Um. How can I help you?"

"My name is Detective Steve Rhines, and I'm looking for Barbee Kingston."

My perfectly-made eyebrows shifted downward. For the life of me, I couldn't understand what he wanted with me. Then it dawned on me something probably happened to Corey.

"I'm Barbee Kingston."

"Can you come with me for a second? I need to speak to you in private."

Amon stepped in. "Whatever you need to say to her can be said in front of me."

Detective Rhines reached behind his back and pulled out a pair of ghetto bracelets. "Barbee Kingston, you are under arrest for the murder and armed robbery of Antonio Shields. You have the right to remain silent. Anything you say can and will be used against you in the court of law."

While detective Rhines continued to read me my rights, everything around me went silent. He stepped behind me and placed the cuffs on my wrists.

"She didn't kill nobody! What the fuck you doing?" Amon shouted.

"You may wanna step back before I arrest you for obstruction of justice."

"Don't worry, B, I'll be down there." Amon frowned and shook his head in disbelief. "Don't say shit to they ass."

Everything around me was moving in slow motion as they escorted me through the crowd. I could feel the stares of the patrons burning a hole through my soul, standing around and staring at me curiously.

On the way out I caught a glimpse of a guy wearing a ball cap, but he had it pulled down low to cover his face. There was something about him that was familiar to me, but I brushed it off. My mind was focused on this crime I didn't commit.

The cop placed me into the backseat of his patrol car and closed the door.

"Take a good look at your club before we pull off," the detective mocked. "You'll be 100 years old before you see this muthafucka again."

I didn't bite the bait. *Fuck saying anything to this bastard!* I reminded myself. But I couldn't help fearing his words might come true.

I sat on the hard plastic seat in discomfort and watched the club get smaller and smaller as he drove me away. Had that bitch named Karma finally caught up to me? I had always heard bloody money was hard to wash your hands of. Now I feared that was about to come true.

But if the detective thought he was going to break Blacque Barbee, he had the wrong bitch.

Chapter 1

Barbee

The patrol car pulled up to the Miami Dade Police Department and came to a complete stop. I watched as Officer Dick eased his Uncle-Tom-ass from the seat. He walked around to my side of the car and opened the door.

"Get outta the car, pretty lips," he smirked. He grabbed me by the arm and pulled me toward him. "You a sexy li'l corrupted bitch." He licked his lips and pressed his crotch against my hips. That shit made my stomach turn. He undressed me with his snake-eyes, and I could feel his dick stiffen. "I would've never fell for your tricks, though."

As bad as I wanted to respond, I couldn't allow my tongue to incriminate me. What I really wanted to say was, *First off, you ain't my type, and ya money ain't long enough to catch the attention of a thoroughbred bitch like me.* In this game called life, we had to pick and choose our battles. Now wasn't the time for a battle so, for the first time, I swallowed my pride, ignoring his slick rap and sexual gestures.

He slammed the door hard as if he read my thoughts, then he snatched me up by the arm and pulled me toward the precinct. I walked slowly past every officer with my head held high and an evil smirk plastered on my beautiful face. My attitude still screamed *the baddest bitch is here!*

The pissed-off officer escorted me to a private room with a wooden table, two chair, and a single tinted Plexiglas window. I prepared myself for a long-ass interrogation. I wasn't telling them shit. After I was un-cuffed, he pulled out my chair so I could sit down.

"The quicker you confess to the crime, the quicker I can go to a place you will never see again." He squeezed my shoulder and smiled. "And that place is called home."

Snatching myself from his grip, I smiled back at him. "That's what yo' mouth say, but I'm going home 'cause I didn't kill nobody."

"That's what they all say until that evidence hits the table." He leaned in closer and whispered in my ear. "Those dyke bitches gon' have a field day with yo' sexy ass. See, you would've been a nice piece of arm candy for a real man, such as myself, but you stuck on that ghetto-ass lifestyle."

This muthafucka's breath smelled like straight ass, and he tried me for the last time. "I would advise you to back up and get your funky-mouth-ass out my face. Yo' breath smell like you been eating ass and sucking dick all night. And I can tell you don't like women with that foul-ass attitude toward me. To be in my presence is a blessing, bitch, so get it right and thank me."

Officer Dick stood erect and frowned at me. "All this coming from the mouth of a hood-rat bitch."

"Ya' mama a hood-rat bitch, and ya' daddy should've made her triflin'-ass swallow ya' gay ass. You would've been one less fuck-nigga I have to deal with."

The way he scrunched up his face told me I struck a nerve. He took one step backward and drew his hand up at me, striking me in the face. "Watch yo' mouth, bitch. My mama dead."

I wasn't fazed by that weak-ass slap. "I don't give a fuck. Fuck yo' mama and that weak-ass slap, bitch."

Before he could say another word, the door slung open and in stepped a well-dressed Caucasian man. "Detective Rhines, what the fuck you doing? Are you trying to bring on charges to the bureau? Get out, now!" he barked.

Without a word, he tucked his tail and followed the orders given to him.

"I'm Lieutenant Taylor, and I apologize for what happened.

If you want to press charges, I understand."

"I'm good," I replied. That bitch slap wasn't enough to make me work with the folks. I believed in street justice because the system wasn't designed to help a bitch like me.

"Okay." The lieutenant walked out and closed the door.

Fifteen minutes passed, and no one had returned to finish questioning me. Just sitting there made me realize a bitch like me was too fine and savage to be sitting in an interrogation room. This was some wild and unimaginable shit. Out of all the years I'd been pulling capers and busting these niggas' domes, I finally found myself jammed up in some bullshit I didn't commit. Was I guilty of robbing and assaulting those clown-ass niggas? Hell yeah. But to murder them without a justifiable cause wasn't my mode of operation. There was no doubt in my mind they had the wrong bitch.

While I collected my thoughts, I rocked back and forth in my seat. It was cold as hell. My arms were covered in chill bumps, and the tip of my nose was cold as ice. They needed to make it snappy with their procedure so they could send me to the county jail, because all they were getting was a *fuck you* from my mouth.

Sudden movement could be heard outside the door, and seconds later the doorknob turned. They were finally joining me once again in the meat locker.

Officer Dick walked in and leaned against the wall. My guess was he got his ass chewed out by the lieutenant. The woman he was with was carrying a folder. She approached me, pull out the chair, and took a seat. "Good evening, Miss Kingston. I'm Detective Burkes, and you've met my partner, Detective Rhines."

My lips didn't part to acknowledge that wig-wearing ho, looking like a bitch's grandma, coming up in here being all formal and shit, like she was on my side. That ho was black as me, but we were definitely not one and the same. Not working for the other side.

Detective Burkes observed the scowl on my face and peeped I wasn't friendly. That made her cut straight to the chase.

"I'm going to assume you know why you're here. I'll skip the introductions, since you don't seem interested. Did you murder Antonio Shields?"

My mean mug tatted on my face was lethal. "I don't know who that is."

The plan was to be mute, but I needed to know who the fuck they were talking about. That name didn't ring a bell at all.

Detective Burkes leaned forward, interlocked her fingers, placing them on top of the table. "Let's not play games here. The quicker you confess, the quicker we can get out of here."

"I'm not confessing to shit because I didn't do shit." I was standing firm on my word to protect my innocence.

"Listen, I can't help you unless you are willing to talk and help yourself. If you don't do that, then I'll make sure I push for the maximum sentence after you're proven guilty in a court of law." She paused, waiting on me to answer. Once she realized I wasn't talking, she continued. "That means you'll never see the light of day again, and you can kiss your club goodbye forever."

This ho was really trying to persuade me into confessing to this bogus-ass murder charge. My name was Blacque Barbee, in case she didn't get the memo. I didn't know what the fuck she thought, but I wasn't going out like that.

"Listen, sis, I didn't do shit. I don't know what you talking about, and I would appreciate it if you get me the fuck out of here so I can carry on with my night."

Detective Dick walked toward us and placed both hands flat on the table. "I don't believe you, and I know for a fact you did it." He spoke slowly, and the sound of his voice sent chills over my body. His eyes were locked onto mine, as if he could see through my soul.

Returning the evil glare, I didn't blink or budge. I needed him to know he couldn't intimidate me. "Well, it doesn't matter what you believe, but what you can prove." A smirk spread across my lips as I hit him with Rich's infamous line.

Det. Burke looked up at her partner while tapping the folder. He nodded his head and smiled. Both of them muthafuckas were working my nerves with all that silent talk. Little Miss Wig smiled back at him before turning her attention back to me and opening up the folder, removing its contents.

Pushing the folder to the side, she removed the photos and spread them across the table in front of me. "Do you recognize the victim now?"

Slowly bringing my head down, I prepared myself to see the worst. My heart was pumping blood faster than an oil rig. If I was going to make it out of here, I needed to calm myself down. I simply stated in my head, *Show no weakness, and never let them see you sweat.* I was very familiar with their tactics. I'd watched The First 48 a million times, and I was well aware of the way they operated. They couldn't offer me a cigarette, water, or a steak dinner to talk. These bastards were trained to sniff guilt out like their K-9s.

Once my breathing was under control, I looked down at the pictures in front of me. The horrific crime scene, printed in color, sucked the air out of me, damn near giving me a massive heart attack. As long as I'd sat and convinced myself I was innocent, that bitch Karma sentenced me to life without a muthafuckin' jury.

Glaring up from the photo in front of me was a blood-soaked bed with a naked corpse on top of the sheets, lying face-down. In the second photo he was lying upright with a sheet sprawled at his waist. I recognized him immediately as Tony, my drunk and aggressive target. A lump formed in my throat, so I swallowed my spit in an effort to push it down. My mind kept telling me, *Stay calm, B. They can't prove shit.*

Allowing my inner self to take control over the situation, I broke my eye contact with his body and looked Detective Burkes dead in the eyes. "I still don't know who that is." I sat back in the chair and folded my arms across my chest. No longer was I cold, because the heat on my ass literally put an end to that shit.

Detective Dick balled up his fist and hit the table. "Barbee, stop the bullshit. We know it's you." He stood erect and paced the floor. "We know you have an accomplice, and all you have to do is drop his name. You can testify against him, and I'll do everything in my power to get you a lesser sentence."

All that was flat-out bullshit. If they had anything on me concrete, I would've gone straight to jail without passing go. This was their way to get me to confess to the crime. And once I admitted to being there, I might as well have pistol-whipped him myself. I was getting the same time as Rich, no matter what.

"Sorry, I can't help you. I still don't know who that is."

"Oh really? I have something that will refresh your memory. So sit tight, and I'll be right back." Detective Burke walked away with her partner on her tail. I couldn't help but wonder what the fuck they had on me.

***

Corey

Seeing Barbee for the first time in months was like a breath of fresh air. She seemed very happy at her grand opening until the folks showed up and slapped the cuffs on. As she was being escorted out, we made eye contact, but I knew she didn't recognize me with the ball cap on. Although we weren't on speaking terms, I would've never missed her grand opening. I knew how much that meant to her, and I wanted to share that special day with her, even if it was from afar. No one knew I was in town, not even Sierra.

After Barbee was walked outside, I slipped through the crowd and followed them into the parking lot. I was in a rental with an out-of-state tag in order to stay low-key. I made sure to keep myself at a distance to ensure they wouldn't notice they were being tailed. Once we made it to the Miami Police Department, I parked my car and watched closely as the officer pushed up on Barbee. My heart told me to get out and check that nigga, but my mind told me to stay calm and not blow up my spot. In due time that bitch-ass nigga would see me.

I waited a good ten minutes before I walked inside to check on my girl. I couldn't risk her seeing me, so I looked around to make sure she was out of sight. There was a lady sitting behind a desk, so I stepped to her.

"Excuse me, I'm here to check on my sister. She was brought in for questioning a little while ago."

She looked up at me. "What's her name?"

"Barbee Kingston."

"Okay, give me a second and I'll check that out for you."

"Thank you." I watched as she walked away and headed in the direction of a female detective. They both looked in my direction before heading my way. "This is Detective Burkes. She'll answer questions you may have."

"Thank you." I extended my hand and she didn't hesitate to grab it.

"How are you, Corey?" she smiled.

The problem with Trisha is we used to kick it for a brief moment, but I cut her off because she was one of those overly independent-ass women. Don't get me wrong, I loved a woman who had her own shit. But when they thought they were too self-sufficient for a man to come in and be *the man*, I had a problem with that. I would dismiss that type with the quickness.

"What are you doing here?"

Seeing a familiar face put me at ease, knowing I would be able to get the information necessary, and quickly, but in order to do that I had to flex the truth a little bit. "A friend of mine was picked up for questioning, and I need to know why and how much is her bond?"

"I see." She looked at me with a questioning stare. "And what is this friend's name?"

"Barbee Kingston."

The sudden shift in her demeanor and frown on her face made it obvious she knew exactly who I was looking for. At that point I knew she would be reluctant to give me what I needed. In fact, I knew she wasn't gonna help me, period, just for the fact it's a female. Needless to say, the bitch was still salty about me curving that ass.

"You sure that ain't your girlfriend?" Trisha folded her arms across her chest.

"Does it matter?" Yep, she was still bitter, so I wasn't about to feed into that bullshit. "She's a childhood friend, and I need to check on her."

"She's in here for second degree murder and armed robbery. I'm afraid she doesn't have a bond."

Those words hit me hard in the chest and I lost my breath. Robbery was one thing, but murder was another. "Murder? Nah, I don't believe that. That's impossible."

"Anything is possible." The bitch acted as if she knew this for a fact.

"Who did she supposedly murder?"

Trisha tooted her nose up. "I'm not at liberty to say. She can tell you, but I can't."

I knew that bitch was lyin'. She was just bitter as fuck. It was cool, though, 'cause I would have all the answers soon enough. "Have a good night." I smiled at her and walked away. It felt like I had the weight of the world on my shoulders, and suddenly I was being held down. My plan was to dip in and out of town, but now leaving was no longer an option. My baby needed me, and it was my job to make sure I did everything in my power to make sure she didn't rot behind those prison walls, even if that meant going to the muthafucka I hated the most. But for Barbee Kingston, I was willing to get in bed with the devil.

Right before I pulled off, I saw Amon and Mercedes pull in.

Destiny Skai

Chapter 2

Barbee

For the first time in a long time, I was a nervous wreck. I found myself shaking my leg like I had restless leg syndrome, and I was even biting my nails. Even my fuckin' palms were sweaty! Whenever they decided to come back to the room, I knew all of that had to stop.

The door swung open, and when Detective Burkes and her sidekick walked in, she had this devilish look on her face. There was something in her hand, but I couldn't make out what it was. As she got closer, she stood to the side of me and placed a cellphone in front of me.

"I have a little something for you. I knew you would be quite the actress, and I must say you deserve and Oscar for that performance you just put on."

The wig-wearing ho hit the button to light up the screen and pressed play on a video. My eyes protruded from their sockets as I watched myself on camera doing the unthinkable. My heart skipped several beats, and at any moment I knew I would pass out from lack of oxygen. All the breathing exercises in the world couldn't slow down my heart rate.

The video footage in front of my face showed me cleaning up behind myself after Rich pistol-whipped Tony. I was caught red handed with my ass out, robbing him for his jewelry and money. Anger took control of my body, because that sneaky muthafucka was recording me the whole time, and I never paid it any attention.

While we were in Tallahassee, that fuck-nigga said he deleted it. I should've known not to trust his ass to get rid of the evidence. From the time he showed me that video, right before he let Mercedes go, he was able to control me with it.

Detective Burke picked up Rich's cellphone and slipped it into her pants' pocket. "Are you ready to talk now?"

I didn't say shit. I just sat there like I was mute.

She slid a pen and a piece of paper across the table. It was a waiver. "Save yourself, Barbee. You seem like a very smart woman. As you can see, Rich is not going to save you. He's already in the department's custody."

Picking up the pen, I twirled it between my fingers, thinking about what she was saying. Rich probably told them everything in order to save himself, but then again, maybe he didn't. I knew how he felt about me, but that was before we tried to kill each other. One thing was for sure: I wasn't going out like that. His ass was the reason I was in this situation to begin with. All he had to do was walk away and let me live my life, but nah, he was too pussy-whipped to do that. He had a wife at home and kids, but no, his greedy ass wanted it all. That was just like a typical nigga.

My decision was final. I pulled the paper close to me and began to write. When I was finished, I slid the waiver back to her and she picked it up. Detective Burke looked over the paper and tossed it. Her anger and frustration was evident. Detective Dick then walked over, picked up the waiver, and read it out loud.

"*Fuck you. I wanna talk to my lawyer.*" He dropped his hand down to his side. "A lawyer is exactly what you need, 'cause you ain't getting out of this." He walked over to me and yelled. "Stand up." When I rose to my feet, he pushed the chair out the way and cuffed me.

"You might as well plead guilty. There's no need in wasting taxpayers' dollars," Detective Burkes added.

The holding cells were gross. I just knew I would break out with some type of infection. Once I was booked after sitting in that pissy-ass cell for two hours, I was fingerprinted and taken upstairs to population with the rest of the females. In my hand I carried toiletries and personal hygiene items – all cheap shit that was guaranteed to make my pussy and underarms itch. This was something I couldn't see myself getting used to. When I finally made it to my cell, I unpacked my things and attempted to make my bed. After struggling for a few minutes, a boyish-looking girl walked into the room.

"Here, let me help you with that."

"Thanks." I couldn't help but notice she looked a lot like the rapper Juvenile.

"This your first time being locked up, huh?"

I smiled. "It's that obvious, huh?"

"Yeah. What's your name?"

"Barbee, but you can call me B."

"Well, nice to meet you, B. My name is Shyne, and it looks like we bunkies. I'm cool and easy to get along with." Shyne paused for a second. "As long as you don't snore."

I couldn't help but laugh. "No, I don't snore."

"There you go, lighten up a little bit. I know how you feeling, but let me tell you, everything will be okay." She nodded her head.

"I surely hope so." Shyne was very helpful and sweet, which was exactly what I needed. I wasn't in the mood to beat a bitch ass just yet, but don't get it twisted, because I would. We spent a lot of time sitting and talking after lockdown. Shyne was very smart, but she couldn't keep her hands off that dope. She said it was because hustlin' ran through her blood. Her daddy did it, and so did her brothers. Then one day her and a friend decided to rob the plug, and it turned out bad. Now she's facing pre-meditated murder and a robbery charge. I saw we had too much in common.

"So, how long have you been locked up?" I could tell she

had been there for a while based on the large amount of supplies stocked up in her room. She appeared to be quite comfortable.

"Twenty-six months."

Damn, I was blown. "Damn, that's a long time to just sit in the county. How do you do it? I mean, it seems like you're fine with it."

"It's called the power of prayer. With God with me, who could be against me? I have faith God will eventually set me free and give me a fresh start."

Before I knew it, time had slipped away and it was lights out. Unaware of the time, I heard loud talking over the PA system.

"Count time, ladies," the bitches in green yelled.

I pulled the wool blanket from over my head to find Shyne looking dead in my face. "What the hell is going on?" I asked.

"It's count time, so hop down."

I was bitchin' 'cause I hated to be awakened from my sleep. "What time is it?"

"Five."

"In the morning?"

Shyne was amused by my reaction. "Yeah, it's shift change, but we can go back to bed after count."

I was livid. "Ugh, I can't do this!"

Shyne helped me get down from the top bunk. Two officers came in, did the count, and walked away. We went back into her room, 'cause I wasn't claiming that shit, and closed the door. Shyne watched me climb back into my bunk. "See, that didn't take long."

"Yeah, now I can go back to sleep." I closed my eyes and thought about how I was gon' fuck Rich up.

Around eight in the morning we were awakened for the

breakfast call. If it wasn't for Shyne, I would've never gotten up for the shit. We stood in a single-file line and grabbed our trays one-by-one. This shit was bogus as fuck.

There was an open area where we could sit and eat, but I opted out of that choice. "Let's go in the room. I hate to sit around a bunch of strange bitches. Staring all in my face and shit."

"Yeah, that's cool wit' me. We can do whatever makes you comfortable."

We sat Indian-style on Shyne's bunk, and I was able to get a good look at the slop in front of me. They served us *powdered eggs* – I was sure about that – grits, sausage, fruit, a biscuit, and milk. Unappealing was an understatement.

"Why you looking like that?" Shyne peeped the mean mug on my face.

"I can't eat this shit." A bitch like me was used to fine dining.

Shyne's laughter was hearty, yet contagious. I couldn't help but to join in. "The Queen of England can't eat that, huh?" she joked.

"This food looks crazy."

Shyne was still laughing. "I swear it's not as bad as it looks."

"Bullshit."

Shyne pulled a plastic bag from underneath the mattress. "I'm 'bouta hook you up."

This fool had all types of condiments, better known as contraband, on hand. I sat back and watched her season the food and add cheese to the grits. "You gon' love this shit. Watch what I tell you."

"I highly doubt that." I wasn't convinced at all. Not even a smidge.

"We'll see." She slid the tray back over to me. "Go ahead.

Try it."

I inhaled so much air and held my breath, while I put the food in my mouth. Chewing slowly, I breathed a little and to my surprise it didn't taste like throw up. The next test was the meat. I used my spoon to break off a little piece. I chewed that slowly, but quickly spit it out into a napkin. I couldn't get with that shit point blank period. That shit tasted like cardboard.

"You a'ight?" Shyne was killing her food like it came from Cracker Barrel or some shit.

"You can have that meat and bread. I'm not eating that."

After breakfast was over, it wasn't a whole hour before some chick walked into the room with her hands on her hips. I knew she didn't want me 'cause I didn't know the broad. She had an orange, short cut that looked like it was supposed to be permed six months ago. That ho looked like a rooster.

"Damn, it ain't been 24 hours and you got a new bunkie already?"

"Man, get out my room wit' that fuck shit. I don't own this muthafuckin' jail, and besides, I don't fuck with you no way."

"What's mine will always remain." She rolled her neck so hard I thought that bitch was gon' fall off.

"Get the fuck outta here. I don't belong to you." Shyne was getting pissed by the second.

"You think I'ma let another bitch come in and take my place?"

I don't know who Foghorn, the rooster from Looney Tunes, thought she was, but she was about to find out real quick I don't play those type of games. My legs couldn't move fast enough to get me off that bunk. I stood to the side of Shyne.

"Ho, let's get one thing muthafuckin' clear: I don't do pussy. I have my own. Whatever y'all got goin' on, leave me the fuck out of it, 'cause I promise you don't want these problems.

26

"Bitch, shut the fuck up, 'cause I wasn't talkin' to you."

Before I knew it, I reached across Shyne and hit that ho dead in her mouth, busting her lip, but it didn't stop there. I was beating the brakes, the carburetor, gas line, and everything else off that bitch. Her li'l entourage was standing behind her, taking notes of the fresh ass-whooping they homegirl got. I left that bitch leaking like a faucet.

***

Rich

I sat across the table from my attorney, dressed in a blood-colored jumpsuit. I had been in custody for the past month, and I wasn't feeling this shit. They had me on a murder and robbery charge, so I wasn't going anywhere.

After I crashed my car into the light post, I was taken back to the hospital I had just escaped from. The impact from the accident left me with a concussion and a broken collarbone. A few days later I was questioned by two detectives about the video found on my phone. I was taken to the Palm Beach County Jail until I was extradited to Miami.

My stare was cold enough to freeze any bitch right now, and my bitch-ass attorney was about to get the business. "Were you able to locate my wife?" I asked through gritted teeth. I already had a feeling what he was about to say.

Adjusting the glasses on his pale, freckled face, he looked away. "No. She's been placed in protective custody, and that means she's at an undisclosed location."

"Okay, so use your fuckin' connections to find the bitch."

He shook his head. "I'm sorry, but that's beyond my job description and way above my pay grade. She's going to testify against you."

"That fuckin' bitch." I hit the table with a closed fist. "You better pull a fuckin' rabbit from ya hat or ya ass. I don't give a fuck where it come from. Find that bitch and silence her."

"She's the least of your worries right now because they have Barbee Kingston in custody."

For some odd reason I was surprised, but I didn't know why. It wasn't like I didn't know it was coming. Maybe it was because it took them a month to finally bring her in. Even though that muthafucka tried to kill me, I still loved her crazy ass. Barbee was a gangsta-ass bitch, and any nigga would be lucky to have her on their arm.

"I'm not worried about Barbee turning state on me. She ain't that type of female. She's a loyal-ass chick. No matter how much she hate me, she ain't gon' talk."

"And what makes you so sure about that?" he asked.

"If Barbee wanted to snitch on me, she would've did it a long time ago."

"Yeah, but the tables have turned. She can turn state on you and get a sentence reduction. I'm trying to protect you as my client. Do you understand that?"

I didn't respond. Instead I tapped my fingers against the table in deep thought. For what it was worth, it was my fault we were in this predicament. I made her lure them sucka-ass niggas in and rob them. It was me who killed the nigga.

"This is what's going to happen." I leaned forward and looked him in the eyes so he would have a full understanding of what I was about to say. "I'm going to take the charges for Barbee. I want her to get full immunity."

Julius placed his hand on his head and took a deep breath. "Do you hear how you sound right now? You want me to get your co-defendant full immunity?" He was acting like he was the muthafucka about to do the time. I already knew I was going away forever, but I couldn't let that happen to her. Giovanni

28

ruined her enough.

"Full immunity and nothing less," I reiterated just in case he didn't hear me the first time.

"Whatever, Rich. It's your life."

"And that's exactly what I'm getting, anyway, so fuck it. I'm paying you, so do what I tell you to do. And if you don't, I will tell the fuckin' judge myself."

"I'll arrange for you to go in front of the judge." Julius opened up his briefcase and pulled out a pen and piece of paper. "Write a letter stating that you wish to take the charges and accept all responsibility for the crimes committed."

I picked up the pen and started to write.

***

Corey

Monday morning rolled around pretty fast, and I had a shitload of things to do. While I was away I caught wind that Sierra was spending all of her time with her punk-ass baby daddy. That hit burnt me to the core, but there was nothing I could do about it now. Dre was the father of my niece or nephew, whether I liked it or not.

Before I headed out to start my day, I stopped by the apartment to make sure Sierra was gone to school. The place was nice and neat, and I couldn't help but wonder if Dre had been inside my spot. I knew Barbee didn't have any beef with him, so she would let the nigga in there on the strength of my sister. After a quick scan of the place, I hit the road.

The Miami Police Department was the last place I wanted to be, but I had to get B out of jail. The love I had for her wouldn't allow me to leave her in that hellhole. That was no place for a woman of her stature.

I was glad the sun wasn't beating a nigga down. The seventy-five degree weather wasn't bad at all. I found a visitor spot close to the building and killed the engine. It was time to go up and see the devil himself.

The receptionist was filing her fingernails when I stepped to the counter. She didn't bother looking up, as if she had some better shit to do.

"I hate to ruin your spa day, but I need to see the Chief of Police."

She finally looked up. "Oh, I'm sorry. I didn't see you there."

"Of course you didn't."

Brushing off what I said, she picked up the phone and placed a call. "What's your name?"

"Corey Belizaire."

"There's a gentleman here to see the Chief." She paused for a brief second before she spoke again. "Corey Belizaire." She repeated, then placed her hand over the receiver. "He's in a meeting right now, but they said to have a seat and he'll be out shortly."

My face balled up instantly. I wasn't on that shit today, so I had to let her know I wasn't fuckin' around. "Tell him who's here and it's an emergency, so he needs to end that meeting right now."

The receptionist snapped her head back and looked at me like I had two heads or some shit. Apparently she didn't know who I was, so I assumed she was new. About two minutes later she hung up the phone. "You can go up now. He's waiting for you." She barely made eye contact with me. I stepped from the desk and made my way to the Chief.

Stepping from the elevator, I walked straight into his office without knocking. The Chief was standing with his hands folded, staring out the window. I closed the door and walked toward his desk.

"You're quite demanding." He turned to face me.

"I guess I got that honest," I smirked.

The Chief pulled out his chair and sat down. "Have a seat."

There were a lot of children's drawings on his desk, so I picked up one and read it out loud. "Thanks for coming to career day, Chief Belizaire. From Mrs. Lawson's fourth grade class." I sat it down and looked up at him. I didn't have to say a word because my silence spoke volumes, and I could sense his discomfort in my stare.

"To what do I owe the pleasure of having my son show up here at my office today?" My sperm donor walked over to his desk and sat down. I couldn't pull myself to call him father because he didn't raise me. "Have a seat, son."

He was one of the most respected men in the community, and they all look up to him. They looked at him and thought *that's the way a real man is supposed to be.* In my eyes he was a coward. He allowed Sierra to be placed into the system and me to be raised by the streets, all because he had a wife who would not accept his illegitimate kids. When our mom died, this muthafucka pulled a Houdini, but it was all good, because he would reap what he had sewn.

"What do you need me to do this time? The only time I hear from you is when some shit went down. By the way, how is Sierra?"

"She's good. I guess you'll be a granddaddy soon. I mean, only if you allowed to."

Chief blinked a few times. "She's pregnant?"

"Yep."

"What is she having?" If I wasn't mistaken, he seemed to be very happy.

"She didn't find out yet."

"How far along is she?"

"Four or five months."

The Chief sat back in his chair with a huge smile on his face. "I want all of us to get together and have dinner as a family."

I shook my head. "There's only one problem."

"And what's that?" he asked.

"We're not a family." And I meant that shit, too.

"Come on, Corey, I'm really trying here. I helped you get her back. I gave you the money, the tax returns, and the lawyer. Please let me make up for lost time. Fuck my wife and how she feels. I let her keep me away from the both of you, and that shit wasn't right. I was younger back then, but I've matured now, and I just want the chance to do the right thing."

The wheels in my head went to spinning full force. I was in deep thought for about a minute. "You abandoned us when we needed you the most."

He held up one finger. "Now, hold up. I never abandoned y'all. I just wasn't there in physical form to raise you and your sister. From day one I gave your mother money. Do you recall your mother having a job? How do you think she provided your food, clothes, and shelter?" He patted his chest. "That was all me. Ask Sierra about Jennifer and David. Better yet, how do you think you got such a light sentence on that murder, or every dope charge you got magically disappeared? Oh yeah, I did that, too."

Now it all made sense as to why my charges were dropped or removed from the system. "Okay, you're right. It's the least I can do. Let me talk to her, and then we can set something up."

"Thanks, Corey. I appreciate that, from the bottom of my heart. I just wish I would've come to my senses years ago."

"You're welcome, and you have plenty of time to make things right. But let's get to the reason for my visit.

For the next five minutes I explained Barbee's ordeal to the

32

Chief, from the arrest, charges, and the two clown-ass detectives on the case. He sat back comfortably in his leather chair, listening attentively.

"I heard about that case. We have her accomplice in custody. His name is Richard Gathers. The both of them are being charged with first degree murder and armed robbery."

"She didn't do it."

The Chief sighed. "I know you want to believe that she's innocent, but she's not. We have her on camera robbing the victim."

Now I was getting' pissed the fuck off. "He kidnapped and beat her, I'm telling you. Check with the hospital and you'll see she was brought in with a lot of injuries last month."

The expression on his face told me he wasn't buying it. "Alright, I'll have someone look into that."

"That's not all, though. She needs a bond. I can't have her in there like that."

"I'll make a call to the judge on her case." He nodded his head. "Is that all?"

"For now. I just want her out and a full investigation done. I'm telling you, he made her do this."

"Okay, I'm on it. I'll call you as soon as I get some details."

I stood up and extended my hand to him for a handshake, 'cause hugging wasn't an option. "Thanks, Chief."

"Pops would suffice," he smiled.

"We ain't there yet."

"Please talk to Sierra. I want to make things right between us."

"Gotcha."

Chapter 3

Sierra

It was my first day of school. I was the new chick on campus, aside from the freshman class. It was my junior year, and I was beyond excited about my new journey. I was fresh to death with my little baby bump, Corey and Dre made sure of that. To make my grand appearance, I rocked an Adidas fit with the matching kicks. To accessorize, I threw in my Pandora necklace, bracelet, and Tory Burch backpack. I was definitely that girl, and the heavy stares confirmed that.

Every group of boys I passed tried to get my attention, but I ignored them while sashaying through the crowd, slangin' my 24-inch Brazilian body wave hair. I couldn't lie, there were some cuties on campus, but my heart belonged to Dre. He was everything to me, and all I wanted him to do was leave Tokee by the time I gave birth to our baby. That was his promise to me, and I believed him wholeheartedly. I wanted to have a little girl since he already had a son with his namesake. Having his first girl would mean so much to him.

On the inside of the school, a majority of the students were hanging out in the commons area. To outsiders, some of these girls looked as if they had just left the club. They were rockin' short skirts, shorts, dresses, and lace fronts. During my fifteen-minute walk, the bell rang, so I made my way to my first period class, Algebra II. The hallways were packed, and many of the students seemed lost. Thank God Dre and I attended orientation, because otherwise I would be amongst that crowd.

The teacher was standing outside the door, sending all of them in the right direction.

"Hello, Mr. McMillian," I greeted him with a pleasant smile.

"Ms. Sierra, how are you?"

I giggled. "I'm surprised you remember my name."

"It's hard to forget a student with a unique personality," he chuckled. "And with the help of orientation being a week ago."

"Good memory." I walked inside the classroom and took a seat in front of his desk. Although I was in a group home, my education was always important to me. And now that I had a baby on the way, I really had to go hard for my little one and secure our future.

The class was damn near full when the final bell rang. Mr. McMillian was closing the door when I heard a student yell. He paused and allowed the tardy girl inside the class. I could tell she was running because she was a little winded. As soon as we made eye contact with one another, her eyes lit up.

"Sierra!" she screeched. Katrina ran over and hugged my neck. "OMG! I missed you so much."

The teacher cleared his throat to get her attention. "Why don't you have a seat next to your friend?"

"I'm so sorry. I'm sitting down right now," she laughed.

After class we compared schedules and found out we had a majority of the same classes together. The first day was always the easiest, so we spent more time talking and catching up during and in-between classes.

"Girl," Katrina popped her lips. "Do you still talk to fine-ass Dre?"

"Yeah, we still together."

"Dang, for real? I thought y'all would've broke up by now."

"Girl, bye. Where he going?" If anyone else would've heard her comment, they would assume he was being shady, but that wasn't the case at all. Katrina and I met in the last group home I was in, and we clicked right off the bat. Our lives were so similar, so that made our bond tighter. She knew everything about Dre since day one. There were a few times I cried on her shoulder.

"Girl, bye. I know how y'all get down, and it ain't nothing nice."

"Well, things have changed now, and we're working on building together."

"Girl, building what?" Katrina sucked her teeth. "A damn paddle boat?"

"Bitch, you tried it!" I rolled my eyes. "A family, stupid." I couldn't wait to shock her with the news.

"Girl, you too young to be a bitch step-mama. Get the fuck outta here with that bullshit."

She was acting very clueless. "If you had a brain, you would be very dangerous. Our own family. I'm pregnant, dummy."

Katrina bounced up and down in her seat. "Ooh, best friend, I'm so happy for y'all. And he better act right, 'cause I'll stab his ass up about you and the baby."

She was always good at making me laugh. "Girl, you know these hands up to date." Katrina caught me off guard when she rubbed my stomach. I smacked her hand away. "Stop before somebody sees you." The commons area was packed for lunch, and I didn't want a bitch in my business.

"I'm sorry," Trina looked around. "I'm sure there's some nosey bitches out here."

"I gotta call Dre to make sure he on time picking me up, 'cause I have a doctor's appointment at 3:30."

Opening up my backpack, I took out my phone and located his number. When *Chocolate Dream* popped up with his picture, I hit the green icon and waited on him to answer.

"What's up, baby?" Dre's voice was low, so I knew that meant he was home.

"Be in front of the school, by the gate at 2:20."

"A'ight, I'll be there," he sounded agitated.

"Why you sound like that?"

"This girl getting' on my fuckin' nerves."

"It's so much easier to leave if you not happy."

Dre exhaled. "I wish it was that simple."

"I'm sure it is, but of course you just making excuses and–"

Dre cut me off. "I'll see you when I get there, 'cause I see where this is going."

"What did I say?"

"You getting' ready to start, and I got enough shit going on over here to be battlin' with you, too. So, I'll see you soon."

"Yeah."

Dre hung up the phone just as the bell started to ring. I put my phone away and we headed to the next class.

"Everything cool?" Trina had a look of concern on her face. "He still coming?"

"Yeah."

***

Dre

As soon as I hung up the phone with Sierra, I opened the bathroom door, and standing in front of me was Tokee. Her arms were folded across her chest, so I knew it was argument time.

Tokee rolled her neck. "Let me guess, that was Sierra, huh?"

"Why do you say stupid shit like that?"

"Hmm, let's see. Maybe because my no-good-ass husband has a baby on the way by a teenage ho."

"Watch ya' mouth, and I'm not gon' keep tellin' you not to disrespect the mother of my child."

Tokee gasped for air. "So, you defending her? I'm your wife, and disrespect any ho that comes between us and tries to

38

fuck up what we had. You a real bitch for that."

Those were the last words she spoke, my hand was around her neck so muthafuckin' fast. I held her midair by her throat. Tokee was petite, so the task was easy.

"Let me tell you something: don't you ever call me a bitch again. I'll kill yo' muthafuckin' ass. And don't disrespect Sierra again. She don't owe you shit. I did. It's not her job to be faithful to you, so if you wanna be mad at somebody, be mad at me. I caused this, not her."

Tokee clutched my hands and tried to speak, but I was cutting off her flow of oxygen. "Dre," she whimpered. The tears in her eyes built up, so I dropped her back on her feet.

"I'm outta here, and don't call me while I'm gone."

During the ride to the school, my mind was all over the place. Feeling confused was not what I bargained for. Here I had Tokee, a sweet, sexy, sophisticated, well-educated, and vibrant woman who could be a spoiled brat at times. She often whined when she couldn't get her way, but I was fine with that because she was used to that type of treatment. She was the last child, and her parents gave her whatever her heart desired, so I expected nothing more and nothing less in her behavior.

Then there was Sierra. She shared some of the same qualities as Tokee, but she was a different type of female. She was very smart, sexy, classy, even as a teen, and a spoiled brat thanks to me. The only difference between the two was Sierra had become dependent because of me. When I met her she was very independent, but after a while I told her she didn't have to want for anything and I would take care of her. I hated the fact she was in a group home, so I promised to move her out of there.

Right before I could move her out, I was robbed by some niggas for the shipment of work that belonged to Tokee's uncle, and from there everything went left, and I had to disappear from her. I hadn't seen or heard from her until my wedding day.

The thing that pulled me close to Sierra was her feisty attitude, smart mouth, and aggression. The way she tried to control me was cute, but she knew when to back down and be a young lady. Not once had she disrespected me or called me out by name, and that's why I wouldn't allow Tokee to disrespect her. Women had it twisted when it came to confronting the woman their man was sleeping with, as if it was her fault we cheated. They should be confronting the man because we were the ones supposed to be committed to them, and not the other way around.

If I chose to be with Sierra, I could train her to be the woman I needed her to be. She would listen to what I told her without a problem. However, when it came to the money tip, I would be the sole provider because she was only in high school. If I lost everything, I would have to start from scratch, but I was okay with that because I was a natural-born hustler. On the flipside of things, Tokee wasn't like that at all. I knew if anything happened to me in the game, Tokee would be that chick who could hold me down and help me bounce back.

The truth still remained that I loved Tokee, but my feelings for Sierra were full blown, and I loved her to the core. *Was it possible to love two women at the same time and be genuine about both?* I thought to myself. But after Tokee called me a bitch that day, I didn't think I could feel the same way toward her anymore. At that very moment I'd lost some respect for her.

I had to shake those thoughts out of my head in order to watch the road and get to where I needed to be on time. The clock on the dash said I had ten minutes to get there. I found Yo Gotti's album CM 9 and let it play so I could clear my mind. The ride to the school was too damn slow thanks to all the damn school zones I had to ride through. I weaved in and out of traffic until I arrived at Piper High and parked outside the fence to wait on her.

Approximately ten minutes later I spotted Sierra walking by the busses with some dude in her ear. I opened the car door and left it running while I met her halfway.

"What's up, baby?" I kissed her on the lips and gripped her ass. Dude was checking out my Balmain fit and my icy-ass jewelry. "Who is this?" I asked.

"Oh, I was just walking her to the end of the sidewalk. We have last period together." I knew he was lying because he was stumbling over his words. Sierra stood there in silence.

"Well, I got my lady from here. Thanks, big dawg." I put my arm around her waist and we walked away.

Sierra laughed. "Baby, you are so petty. Why did you do that?"

"To let that young-ass nigga know you got a man, and he don't have shit to offer you. Now, let's go check on my baby and see how he or she doin'."

"I already told him that, so you ain't got nothing to worry about."

"Oh, I ain't worried, 'cause I'll bury both of y'all asses together and raise my baby solo. Now, try me and think I'm playin'." I opened the car door for her and closed it before going back to the driver side.

We spent an hour and some change in the doctor's office, and afterward I took my baby out to eat. She was craving seafood, so I took her to Red Lobster. This girl ate so much food she made my stomach hurt just looking at her. I hated to end our day together, but I had money to make. My family came first, so I had to make sure I secured the bag before my little princess arrived. Sierra was five months, so I still had some time to get myself together and be there the way she wanted me to.

"I'm not ready to go home yet," Sierra whined.

"I know, baby, and believe me, I'm not ready to leave you yet. There's money to be made, and I have to make sure everything is in order before the baby arrives. Even after she gets here, I still have to work, but it won't be as much like now. You're about to be a first-time mother, and I need to help you as much as possible."

"Okay." I could sense she wasn't happy with my answer, but she knew debating me wasn't the right thing to do.

Sierra kept looking at me with this hunger in her eyes. I had been with her long enough to recognize that stare. I heard the click from the seatbelt, so I glanced a little to the right and observed her licking her lips before leaning over to the driver's side.

"What you doing?" I asked.

"About to suck my dick," she moaned. The seduction was thick in her voice, causing my dick to jump. Sierra unbuckled my belt and pants and slipped her hand into my boxers, awakening the sleeping giant. "This muthafucka so pretty, I can suck it all day." Stroking it up and down, she spit on the tip and stroked it until it reached the full nine inches. Slipping her lips on the tip sent a tingle down my spine. I looked down as she made it disappear into her mouth, inch by inch, and I felt the back of her throat.

"Shit." I squeezed the steering wheel tight and damn near closed my eyes. The only motion that could be seen was her head going up and down in my lap. Using my right hand, I grabbed a handful of the hair I paid for and guided her pace.

"Mm, yeah. Suck yo' nigga dick, just like that." Forcing her head down further, she gagged, but she continued to swallow that meat like I taught her. She was easy to teach because she was about pleasing her man, and that's what I loved about her.

Tokee wasn't on giving a nigga head. I had to ask for the shit and when she did it, it was bad as fuck. She made it known she didn't want to do it. Sierra used every opportunity she had and kept in there without me ever having to ask.

I could feel her jaws lock like a pit bull around my piece. That shit made a nigga toes curl. Lifting her head up, she backed up off it and spit on it once more, licked it off and swirled her tongue around my throbbing head. Thrusting my hips upward, I forced her head back down and hit them tonsils, looking for that gagging sound.

"Damn, I love you." She had me in my feelings like a bitch. "I swear, I'll kill you if you suck or fuck another nigga. This my pussy and mouth. Do you hear me?" With a mouth full of dick it was hard to speak, but she nodded her head to let me know she understood me.

My grip on her hair tightened as the tingling sensation surfaced, indicating a nut was on the way.

"Grr," I grunted. "I'm bouta bust in ya' mouth."

"Go 'head," she mumbled.

Seconds later I let off the first round. That shit had me weak as fuck. Sierra sat up and gargled it, making bubbles. "Swallow it."

I loved to see her do that freaky shit. "Take them pants off and get that pussy wet for me." I pulled into the parking lot of her apartment complex and parked in the back.

"We can go inside."

"Nah, 'cause I gotta leave soon, and if I come in there all I'ma do is sleep in the pussy and miss this money."

My dick was still out and ready for part two. "Come sit on this dick." I adjusted my seat until it would go no further and lifted the steering wheel. Sierra pulled off her pants and climbed over to the driver's seat, mounting my lap. I rubbed the tip across her slit, tickling her pearl, and I could feel her juices leaking. Easing my dick inside, I gripped her hips and pushed her down on it.

"Ah," she cried out. With no mercy, I plunged in and out of her pussy.

"Damn, this muthafucka warm." I was breathing hard. "I meant what I said. You better not give my pussy away. You belong to me."

"I won't," she promised. "I love you too much."

"Say you mine."

"I'm yours," she complied.

"You belong to me?"

"Yes."

"Tell me, then." I continued to stroke like I was trying to dig open a new lining.

"I belong to you. This your pussy. Fuck me hard," she screamed.

Putting my hand around her throat, I dipped in and out of her. Sierra's eyes were closed, and she was biting the hell out of her lip. "I'm about to cum."

"You better be tellin' the truth, 'cause I'll kill you and your brother."

Ten minutes later I was still smashing that ass until I came once more. Releasing my grip on her throat, I grabbed the back of her neck, pulled her close to me and kissed her hard in the mouth. "I love you, baby. We gon' be together, I promise."

"I love you, too, baby."

"How much money do you have left?"

"Sixty."

"Get up and get those wipes out the glove box." I reached in my pocket and pulled out a stack. Whenever I stepped away from the house, I never carried more than a grand. Peeling off two crisp hundreds, I handed them to her. "Here's some lunch money, fat girl."

"Thank you, baby."

After we cleaned ourselves up, we kissed one last time and I drove her to the front of the building. Once she was inside, I pulled off and went to pick up some drops from Boca Raton.

Destiny Skai

Chapter 4

Corey

It was after six o'clock before I finally heard the door unlock. I had been sitting there thinking about everything the Chief said about B. Sierra walked through the door with a huge smile on her face. She ran over and hugged me.

"When did you get back?" I could hear the excitement in her voice.

"Today," I lied. "Where you been? With Dre?" I knew the answer already, but I had to ask anyway.

"Yes. He took me to my doctor's appointment and then out to eat."

I nodded my head. "I see. That's why your hair messed up like that?" The back of her head was a little fuzzy and out of place.

Sierra rubbed the back of her head. "No. I had my head leaning back on the headrest. Why is your mind always in the gutter? That's not all we do, thank you."

"I know Dre very well."

"I haven't seen you in months, so can we please talk about something else? Such as where you been and what's going on with my sister?" She sat down next to me.

I used that moment to look into her eyes and see what'd been going on. "Has he been treating you good?"

"As a matter of fact, yes, he has. For back-to-school he gave me $2,000 and let me drive his car to go shopping."

"Did you spend all the money I sent you?"

"No. I didn't need to. Dre has been taking very good care of me since you left."

That made me happy on the inside that he didn't abandon her, but I wasn't about to tell her that. Maybe he was gon' be a stand-up father after all, and I wouldn't have to kill him.

"That's good to hear."

"Now, can you tell me where you've been?"

"There's so much that's happened, and it's really on a need-to-know basis."

"And let me guess, I don't need to know, huh?"

"What I will tell you is that I've been in Tennessee since I left. The things that happened between us was too much for me to deal with, so I needed to get away for a while."

"And it was that bad that you had to flee across two states to think about it."

It made sense what she was saying, but she would never understand how hurt I was when I found out the truth and nature of B's relationship with Rich. Her fuckin' another nigga was low and unacceptable. She ripped a nigga whole heart out his chest.

"Believe it or not, it was just that bad."

"Were you with a female?"

The look on her face was confirmation she was serious about her questions. I wanted to lie to her, but I couldn't pull myself to do it. I'd been lied to, and I knew how it felt. "I didn't go up there with a female, but I did meet one while I was there through my homeboy."

"Corey, you cheated on Barbee. How could you do that to her? She loves you more than life itself." Sierra's voice cracked, and I knew she was on the verge of crying.

"It's not like that. My nigga always told me I was welcomed in his home whenever I needed to get away, and that's where I went. He saw the state of mind I was in, so he had his girl introduce me to one of her girls. I slept with her a few times, but my guilt was killin' me, so I backed away from her."

"Excuse my language, but that's fucked up, Corey. You should've never did that. You saw what I went through with

48

Dre. How do you think Barbee is going to feel?"

"She won't find out."

"So, you're not going to tell her?"

This girl was givin' my ass the third degree. I knew she loved Barbee, but damn, she was my sister at the end of the day. "I don't know if we'll ever get back together."

"Well, don't bring nobody else around, 'cause I'll never like the bitch."

"Let's change the subject." Discussing B was not what I had planned. "Did you ever receive money from a David Smith while you were in the group home?"

"Yeah, I did, but he never came to see me."

"And did you live with a lady name Jennifer?"

"Yeah. That's where I met uncle David."

The Chief wasn't lying after all. For confirmation, I pulled out my cellphone and showed her a picture of our father. "Is this Uncle David?" I asked.

She nodded her head up and down. "That's him. He used to come and bring Aunt Jennifer money and food for me. When I was 10 she passed away from cancer, and I was placed in a group home. After that I never saw him again, but he always sent me money. On my 14th birthday he sent me clothes, shoes, and a debit card through my caseworker. She said she knew him."

"Well, he wants to see you, but his name is not David, and he's not your uncle."

Sierra looked confused and tilted her head. "Well who is he?"

I took a deep breath. "He's our father."

"What? How?" Her eyes stretched wide and she shook her head. "I'm confused, 'cause this not making any sense."

I watched her as she got up and paced the floor with her hands behind her back. "He was married when he met mommy and got her pregnant. His wife couldn't have kids, so when she heard about us she told him he couldn't see us."

"All this time I've been wondering about him. Now it all makes sense. That's why he would never take me out in public or take me shopping himself."

"He's the Chief of Police in Miami."

Sierra just stood there and stared at the wall. I knew everything I said threw her for a loop, but I was going to make sure she was okay, as I'd done up to now.

Later on that night I was still a little upset, so I hit Amon up. "What's up, bruh?" Amon answered.

"Chillin'. Where you at wit' it?"

"I'm at the crib, sitting in the parking lot, debating if I should go in or not."

"Yo' girl trippin' again?"

"Hell yeah. She on one 'cause I came in late last night."

"Nah, don't go in. I'm back, and I need to get out for a few and talk about this shit with B."

"You know she locked up, right?"

"Yeah I know. That's why I need you to meet me at the strip club, so I can unwind and get this shit off my chest."

"I'm wit' that."

"Meet me at Vegas. I'm headed out there now."

"Bet."

It took me all of twenty minutes to get there, but Amon still wasn't there yet, so I decided to go in without him and wait. I walked through the double doors and paid my admission. The crowd was decent for a Monday night. As soon as I sat down, I was approached by the waitress.

"Hey, what can I get for you?" Shorty was smiling hard as fuck.

"Bring me a bottle of Belaire Rosé."

"Don't you wanna know the price?" This chick was pulling my card, no doubt, so I needed to show her what type of nigga was in her presence. I dug deep in my pockets, pulled out a heavy bankroll, and showed it to her.

"Do it look like I give a fuck about a price?"

"Oh, I'm sorry. I was just asking 'cause we get a lot of cheap niggas in here."

"Well, I ain't one of them niggas. Now, can you go and get my bottle, and a bottle of Hennessey with that?"

That ho had a lot of nerve insulting a boss-ass nigga like me. I ain't nothin' like her baby daddy, ol' fuck-ass ho. I normally didn't degrade women and talk to them like that, but this shit with Barbee had a nigga on beast mode.

It took Shorty ten minutes to come back with my shit. "Here you go." She was trying to keep the smile on her face, but she acted like it was a struggle to be so phony. "That's one fifty."

I gave her two hundred dollars. "Keep the change."

"Thank you." Then she stomped off. I knew she felt like I insulted her, but I didn't give a fuck.

By the time I fixed my cup and started to drink, I spotted Amon walking in my direction. I raised my arm so he could see me.

"What's up, fam?" He dapped me, then sat down and fixed himself a drink.

"Stressin'."

"About B?"

"Hell yeah. You already know."

"Cuz, g'on, be straight."

"I don' know, bruh. They got her on tape robbing the nigga while he was bleeding out his head. This shit crazy as fuck."

"If the shit go to trial, we gotta find that nigga wife, 'cause I know she'll testify against his ass, along with Mercedes."

"Yeah, but she still might get some time."

"We just gotta hope for the best, you know what I'm sayin'?"

"Yeah, man." I took another sip from my cup.

"Where the fuck you been at, nigga? You left a nigga out here solo and shit."

"I had to get away for a while and get my head right. That shit fucked with a nigga pride. I did right by that girl, man, and she was fuckin' another nigga. Not once did I hit another bitch, and I could've on several different occasions."

"So, where did you go?"

"I slid up to Tennessee and fucked with Rod for a few. He showed a nigga a good time."

"How that nigga doin'?"

"Livin' lovely up there. That shit dirt cheap up there. A nigga can live like a king for a little of nothing."

"You livin' like one now."

"Yeah, but the cost of living up there mad cheap."

"I feel you on that. Florida will peel a nigga hat back."

"On my mama, nigga." I laughed for the first time in a long time.

"You know you missed her grand opening?" Amon sipped his drink and waited on a response.

"I was there. You know I wouldn'ta missed that for the world. I was lurking in the back until I saw the detective come in and snatch her up. I followed them to the precinct and all."

"Damn, and you ain't say nothing to a nigga?"

"Nah, I didn't want my presence to be known just yet. That's why I called you to come out tonight."

"I see."

Me and Amon kicked back and chilled for a little over an hour. The stripper chicks kept coming up asking for dances, but

I wasn't on that. I kept turning them away. Besides, I wasn't 'bout paying a bitch bills who I wasn't fuckin'.

Amon was crackin' up. The stripper who was giving him a dance laughed, too. "Bruh, chill out and get a dance, man. You trippin'."

"Nah, I'm straight. Do ya thang."

Amon whispered something in the girl's ear, and she got up and walked to where I was sitting.

"Come on, daddy. I can make you feel better." She started to dance, but it didn't do nothing for me.

"I'm straight. Go back over there and dance for that nigga."

"Don't be like that. Let Candi make whatever on your mind disappear."

I kept trying to get her off, but she was mad aggressive, and it was pissin' me off. "Get the fuck off of me." Using all my strength I pushed her ass so hard she flew into the table and hit the floor.

Amon jumped up and helped her. "Bruh, you trippin', man."

"Fuck that ashy, weave-wearin'-ass ho. I told her to stop. I don't want funky pussy juice on my jeans and shit."

Once she was on her feet, she stared me down. "You gon' regret that."

"Get the fuck outta here, dusty-ass bitch."

Fifteen minutes later security walked over to where we were sitting with the ho I pushed standing behind him. My instincts told me to stand up.

"I'm afraid I have to ask you gentlemen to leave."

"For what? 'Cause I told that ho I didn't want a dance, and she tried to get in my lap anyway."

"There's no need to disrespect the dancer, sir."

"Fuck that ho." I was so heated. The beast inside me said spit in her face, but I had never been that disrespectful, so I let it go.

Amon was on his feet as well. "We good, man. Bruh, let's hit it."

Before I walked away, I looked down at both bottles, and there was still some alcohol left. I picked up both bottles and poured them onto the floor before dropping them all together. Too bad them bitches didn't break. I looked the security guard up and down. "You won't sell shots from my bottle, pussy-nigga."

He didn't say a word while he escorted us to the door. Barbee had a nigga on ten, ready to slap every ho for the shit she pulled on a real nigga.

Amon and I stood outside by my car for a few minutes, just choppin' it up.

"A'ight, bruh, I'm 'bouta head to the house, 'cause this girl blowin' my shit up right nah."

"Go handle ya business and I'll fuck witcha later."

We dapped up one more time and went our separate ways. My head was hurtin' from all that damn liquor, and I had to piss like a muthafucka. I couldn't go back inside and the gas station was too far, so I pulled to the back of the building to take a quick piss. It was dark as fuck, but I had my strap. As I stood on the side of the car, I peeped a set of headlights coming in my direction slowly. I was trying to hurry up, but that was hard to do when you pissy drunk. That shit take long as fuck. I kept my eyes on the car. My left hand was on my dick, and my right hand was on that banger.

"Keep it movin', 'cause I swear you don't want these problems," I said to myself.

The car came to a complete stop and the window came down. I took a good look inside, and it was the stripper ho wit' a nigga.

"That's the nigga right there, bae. Didn't I tell you, you was gon' regret that shit, pussy-nigga?"

Dude stepped from the car and walked around. I could see he had a piece, but I played it cool. I waited until he was in front of his car before I pulled my heat and dumped two slugs in his chest.

His bitch screamed.

The bitch let the window up, but she must've thought I couldn't touch her. I shot through the window and put a single bullet in her brain. Her shit exploded like a melon. Brain matter splashed all over the dashboard and window. I went back to her nigga and put one in his forehead to make sure the nigga was dead.

Running back to the car I jumped in and peeled off. It was time to get the fuck out of dodge.

Chapter 5

Barbee

Since the fight I had with the chick, she hadn't bothered Shyne at all. She wouldn't even look in her direction. We were sitting on the bed playing tunk when I heard my name being called over the intercom.

"Kingston, you have an attorney visit. Kingston, you have an attorney visit."

I was looking crazy because I didn't have an attorney as of yet. Mercedes said she would handle that. I guess she moved faster than I anticipated.

"Why you looking crazy? Get up and go see what they talkin' 'bout. Put on your shirt."

I grabbed my blue uniform shirt and pulled it over my head before I headed to the door. There was an officer standing there, waiting on me.

"Pop the door," she yelled. The door clicked and she pulled it open, backing up so I can walk through. "I have to cuff you until we get there."

I nodded my head, but I didn't respond. This was something I could never get used to. The officer cuffed me from the front, and I was glad about that. Being cuffed from behind was too uncomfortable. Once we made it to the designated area, she removed the cuffs and closed the door behind me to give us some privacy.

"Hello, Ms. Kingston. I'm Tamela Bryant, your attorney."

"Hello." I moved closer to her and sat down at the table. She took me by surprise because I wasn't expecting it to be someone who looked like me. We were damn near the same complexion, she rocked a flat wrap, and she was very pretty.

"Well, the first thing I need to do is to discuss your case."

Ms. Bryant started to shuffle through some papers.

"I don't mean to be rude, but I need to know who sent you before I start volunteering information. Was it my sister?"

"No. I don't know your sister."

"Well, who sent you? I'm not talking until you tell me."

"Let's just say you're receiving help from a man in a very high place."

"Yeah, yeah, I know, God makes everything possible, but who sent you?" This bitch was really irritating me, especially when she started laughing like something was funny.

"Yeah, that's true, but I'm not talking about him."

"Well, who is it?" This made me think the bitch was getting a kick out of this guessing game.

"John Doe."

"I don't know him."

"Of course you don't, but I knew that already." She sat back in her seat. "Anyway, let's talk about your case and your role in the murder and robbery."

She tried me for the last time, so I stood up and walked away. "I'm not talking to you about shit. I'm going back to my cell."

"I know all about your case. The kidnapping that involves Rich, the video, your hospital visit after he tried to kill you and your sister. I know everything, and if you want to get out of here, I advise you to sit down. If you want to do a life sentence, or even worse, the death penalty, then go back to your cell."

Hearing her provide those details had my mind wondering. I stood in place, frozen, staring at the door. Now I really needed to know who the fuck sent her and told her all my fuckin' business. For some reason the first person who came to mind was Rich.

***

Dre

"You picking me up from school today?" Sierra smiled at me on facetime.

I was sitting in front of Louie's house, who is Tokee's uncle. A new shipment was due to come in, so I had to be on top of that. "It depends on how long it takes me to handle this business."

"Ugh." She poked her lip out and rolled her eyes.

"Come on, bae, don't start that. You know I would come if I could."

"Yeah, yeah."

"How can I take care of you and the baby if I don't make money?"

"I know that, but I get out in two hours, and you telling me you might not be finished. That don't sound right."

"Come on, man, stop it. I ain't doing nothing that ain't related to money."

"I'm not a man, and I don't know that."

"You know what I mean. Stop acting like a baby when you about to have one. That's how you gon' act when she get here?"

"Yep, if you keep acting like this."

I couldn't do shit but laugh, 'cause this girl was buggin' big time. Just watching her pout was a comedy show. She was cute when she did it, though. "I swear, you are so dramatic."

"And you are so full of it." Sierra looked away from the screen and put her head down. "You always doing this to me, putting me last. I knew you didn't care about me."

If I didn't know any better, I would've thought she was crying, but I was hip to her game. This wasn't the first time she pulled this on me.

"Sierra, get up and stop playin'." That heffa didn't move. I had to ask her several more times before she finally got up. Looking at her on the screen, I could see her eyes were actually red and wet. "What you crying for?"

"You don't love me."

"You know I love you." When I looked up, I could see one of Louie's workers standing on the porch. He waved his hand for me to come in. "I gotta go, baby, but I'll be there when you get out, in the same spot, okay?"

Sierra finally smiled. "Okay. I love you."

"I love you, too."

Sierra knew how to get me to bend for her, and I'd do it again if I had to. Finally stepping from the car, I walked up on the porch and gave him some dap.

"What's good, my dude?" he asked.

"Shit, I can't call it." Placing my hand on the knob, I turned it, but I didn't open it. "Whe'e Louie at?"

"Back room."

"A'ight."

There was nobody else here, so I didn't know what type of meeting he had going on. When I made it to the back of the house, he was sitting on the couch watching a gangsta movie and smoking a cigar.

"What's up, Louie?"

"I don't know, you tell me." He flicked the ashes off the tip into the ashtray.

Something about him seemed off, but this nigga was wishy-washy, so it ain't no tellin' what the fuck was wrong with this nigga. "Shit, I'm trying to get this money. So, what's up with the shipment?"

"It'll be here in a few days. I'll let you know when it's ready."

"That's what's up. Where is everybody else? I thought you wanted to have a meeting."

Louie took a pull from his cigar and blew the smoke up in the air. The coldness in his eyes was a look I saw before, but this time around I wasn't aware of anything that went left. Everybody paid their money, and all the bricks were sold, so I didn't know what this was about.

"I called a private meeting for me and you 'cause I don't need nobody else in our business. This is family business, feel me?"

"Talk to me. What's going on?"

"First, let me ask you a question." He paused and took another pull from his cigar. "How is my niece doin'?"

"She good."

"You treating her good?"

"No doubt. What's up with the questions, though?"

"When I started selling dope as a teenager, I was given the best piece of advice by the cat that put me on. He told me lying was done with words, but also in silence. I listened to what he said, but I didn't quite comprehend it." Louie sat his cigar in the ashtray. "It wasn't until my money came up missing from underneath my mattress. I ranted and tore the house up from top to bottom. The entire time I did this, my brother was quiet during the whole ordeal. He never said a word and he didn't help me find it. A few days later, I found out it was him that stole my money. You catch my drift?"

"Yeah." I didn't know what the fuck he was talking about, but I agreed with him, anyway. I understood the message, but I didn't understand the point of it.

"Do you remember when you were robbed and cost me 500 grand?" I nodded my head. "We had an agreement I would forgive your debt if you married my niece and treated her like the queen she is because she cherishes the ground you walk on."

"And I've done that."

"Yeah, you married her, but you not treating her good. You

treatin' her like a random bitch from the streets."

I shifted in my seat just in case I needed to put a slug between his eyes. Now I knew where this conversation was going.

"My niece told me about your girlfriend and unborn child." He stood up. "And that's not sitting too well with me, because now you are not a man of your word."

"Let me just say this: before I married Tokee, I was cheating with this chick, but when we made the agreement, I ended things with her. I didn't find out she was pregnant until after the wedding."

"You should've made her have an abortion."

"It was too late, and even if it wasn't, I couldn't force her to do it."

"This what's gon' happen: you gon' end things with her for good and let her raise that child on her own. Give her some money and make her disappear."

Now I was looking at him like he was stupid if he thought that was gon' happen. "Nah, I can't do that."

Louie pulled his cellphone out. "Hold on, give me a second." I watched as he did something in his phone. When he was done, he showed it to me. It was a picture of Sierra.

"That's her, right? If you don't do it, then I will. I'll make sure she disappears for good, and you'll never see her again unless you look at her obituary."

When his final words left his lips, I pulled out my gun and aimed it in his face. "Fuck, nigga, that's the quickest way to sign yo' death certificate." I gritted my teeth 'cause I was two seconds away from peelin' his cap back. "You must've lost yo' muthafuckin' mind if you think I would let you and Tokee keep me away from my child."

Louie's laugh was cynical as he looked at me without a sense of fear. "I see you love her, but if you pull that trigger, your precious little teenager will die right along with me. I have someone outside of her school right now, waitin' on the order to execute." I searched his face for the truth. "Don't believe me? Watch this."

He dialed a number and put it on speaker. "Louie, everything copasetic over there?"

"I have a gun in my face right now," he replied.

"Yo, Dre, put that shit down befo' shit get real ugly in front of shorty school. I don't wanna do it, but I will if you force my hand."

As bad as I wanted to pull that trigger, I had to make sure Sierra was safe, just in case he wasn't bluffin'. Slowly I lowered my strap and let my arm fall to my side. My hands were tied at the moment, and I couldn't do shit, but he was gon' pay for his actions real soon. I needed a plan, and I needed one like yesterday, so I turned and walked away in order to set my plan in motion.

"He walked away. Leave the girl alone."

"A'ight."

"Dre, don't forget what I said," he shouted. "I'll send you a little reminder, just in case you do."

A few seconds later my phone alerted me I had a text message. I thought it was Sierra texting me, but it was Louie. He sent me a picture of her as a reminder to not see her anymore.

On my way to Piper High, I tore the highway up trying to get to Sierra. The only thing on my mind was keeping both of my babies safe. Tokee would be dealt with later.

When I made it to the school, there wasn't a single soul in sight. I checked the time on my watch, and I still had another hour and some change before dismissal, so I left to go and book us a room. It would help kill the time. The navigation said the nearest hotel was 15 minutes away on Commercial Boulevard, so that was where I went. The Comfort Suites wasn't my favorite hotel, but today it would have to suffice.

Check-in didn't take long being that the lobby was empty. The clerk gave me the keys, and I was on my way. Before I went back to the school, I made a quick mall run into Macy's and picked Sierra up a fit and undergarments to wear the next day. We were going to spend the night at the hotel, so there was no point in taking her home to pick up any clothes. I kept an overnight bag in my trunk for the both of us since disappearing together was something we did quite often.

By the time I made it back to the school, the bell had already rung because the campus was flooded with students. I parked in my regular spot and got out the car to look for her. Five minutes later she could be seen walking toward the fence. I greeted her with a hug and a kiss. She was grinning hard as fuck.

"Yo' ass happy as hell now." I grabbed her hand and escorted her to the car.

"You know how I get."

"Yo' ass crazy."

"Crazy about you."

When we arrived at the hotel, Sierra looked around, and then in my direction. "What we doing here?"

"I got us a room for the night." I pressed the button and killed the ignition.

"Oh, you not going home?"

"Nah. I wanna spend time with you, and feed the baby, of course." I winked at her and rubbed her small belly. "Grab that bag out the backseat."

She reached behind her and picked up the Macy's bag. "But I don't have any clothes for school tomorrow."

64

"What you think that is in your hand?"

Sierra peeked inside. "Aw, baby, thank you."

"You don't have to thank me. I'm just takin' care of my responsibilities, like I'm supposed to."

"Well, I appreciate that."

"Come on, let's go."

We ordered food from Golden Crust through Uber-eats and talked for hours about our future together. Although I was married to Tokee, the woman who was carrying my child had my heart. I never wanted to hurt her again or wipe away that beautiful smile on her face. Whenever we were together, she was happy and didn't care about what I had or the material things I could buy her. All she wanted was me.

"Sierra," my voice cracked a little.

"Yes, my love?" Her voice was so angelic when she was happy, and it melted my heart every time.

"I just want you to know I love you beyond the moon and the stars. I fell in love with you the first day we met. I never loved anyone the way I love you, not even Tokee. I would kill for you and protect you until my last breath." I paused for a second. She had me in my feelings. "You got my soul. I promise. And no matter what happens, don't ever doubt my love for you."

She grabbed my hand. "Baby, I love you, too, and I'll do anything for you. All I ever wanted was to be with you. Is everything okay, Dre? You making me nervous."

I leaned over and kissed her lips gently.

That night I made slow, passionate love to Sierra with Bryson Tiller's *Exchange* on repeat, like I would never feel the inside of her again. With every stroke I made, our connection became stronger and stronger. Her soft moans were like a sweet melody in my ears. A stream of fresh tears could be seen traveling down toward her ears.

"I love you so much, Dre," she cried, squeezing me like she never wanted to let go of me.

"I love you, too, baby."

My lips covered her mouth, silencing her cries. We went round for round, losing count until five in the morning.

Chapter 6

Sierra

It had been two weeks since I heard from Dre. The last time was the morning he dropped me off at school after we left the hotel. When I tried calling him that afternoon, he didn't answer the phone, and he wasn't waiting for me after dismissal. To say I was crushed was an understatement. I was angry, pissed, and heartbroken. For the past fourteen days I'd cried myself to sleep every night listening to *Exchange* and wondering if he was okay or what he was doing. The last time he dipped out on me he was walking down the aisle. I could only imagine what he was doing or if something bad happened to him. All I remembered him saying was, *No matter what happens, don't ever doubt my love for you.*

For the past two days I hadn't been to school. I lied and told Corey I was sick, so he gave me a pass. The baby was kicking constantly, and I wanted to share these special moments with him. That night kept playing over and over in my head, and I couldn't understand how he could walk away from me like this. Dre sat there and poured his heart out to me right before he vanished without a single goodbye.

This pain was the worst. I wouldn't even wish it on my most hated enemy. The marriage hurt altogether, but this time it was different. I was pregnant, and I knew for a fact he loved me. In the past it was questionable, but now I was certain he did.

The baby was doing full circles in my belly like her ass was on a jungle gym. I placed my hand on top and rubbed her slowly, the same way Dre did when we lay in bed together. The constant memories we shared tumbled down on me at one time, and I was in tears, snot bubbles and all. There was a knock on the door. I knew it was Corey, so I pulled the covers over my face right before he walked in.

"Hey, you hungry?" he asked.

"No." I tried my best to sound normal.

"Are you okay?" I could see him walking toward me.

"Uh-huh," I replied.

Corey walked over to me and pulled the covers back, revealing my tear-drenched face. "Why are you crying?"

"Nothing."

"Don't lie to me. What the fuck did Dre do to you?"

I was too hurt and embarrassed for Corey to find out he was right about Dre the whole time, so I ignored his question.

"You might as well tell me, 'cause I'm not leaving until you do."

We sat in silence for ten minutes before I opened my mouth. It was clear to me there was no other way around it, so I gave in. "I haven't seen or heard from him in two weeks, and I don't know what to do." I broke down and just let it flow. Corey moved closer to me and pulled me into his arms. While I cried on his shoulders, I explained every detail about our last night together and how he just up and disappeared after that. He kissed me on the top of my head.

"Don't you worry, I'm going to handle Dre. I want you to save those tears for his funeral, 'cause it's coming soon."

"Corey, please don't kill him," I begged.

"Why not? You think he out here crying over you?" He let me go and grabbed my chin with his hand. "I gave that nigga his final warning months ago, and he still tried it. He disrespected me for the last time."

Corey got up and left my room, closing the door behind him. I cried harder 'cause I knew he meant every word he said. Dre was gonna die if he wasn't dead already.

***

Corey

When I fought to get my sister, I never expected any of this to go down. I figured there would be some issues with boys, but not a grown-ass man, and someone I was once close with at that. It didn't matter if we grew up together or not, that nigga had to go.

I pulled up to his hangout spot, but I didn't see his car. All the niggas that were posted up I knew from the hood, so I jumped out of the car and approached them.

"What up, y'all boys?" They all dapped me up. "Y'all seen Dre?"

"Nah, he ain't been around for a minute now. I heard some shit popped off between him and Louie." No matter what went on in the hood, Pete always had the details.

"Is that right?"

"Yeah, that's what the streets say." Pete was smoking on a cigarette.

"Well, if y'all see him, let him know I'm looking for him."

"A'ight, fam."

"A'ight. Y'all boys be easy."

After I left the spot, I rode around to a few places he was known to hang out at, and also by his crib, but this nigga was nowhere to be found. I wasn't ready to take it in yet, so I slid up on Amon at the gambling spot. They were in that bitch shooting dice.

"What's up, bruh?" We G-hugged. I spoke to the other dudes present. "I need to holla at chu for a second," I whispered to Amon, making sure no one else heard me.

When we were out of earshot, I let him know the deal between Sierra and Dre. Amon nodded his head.

"I see he on that fuck shit."

"I'm about to put an end to all of that. I need you to get up with yo' shooters and let 'em know it's a bounty on that nigga head. I'm paying ten bands for anybody that deliver him to me, dead or alive."

"I'm on it, fam."

We shook hands and sealed the deal. All I had to do was wait on that call.

***

Barbee

Today was the day I went in front of the judge to determine if bail could be set. I was happy as hell to be going, but not with the dumbass process. First off, they woke me up at four in the morning when court didn't start until nine. That alone was a deal breaker for me, but hey, whatever it took to get me out, then I was all for it. If the judge granted me a bond, I was prepared to get myself out. Mercedes said she would pay it, but I couldn't have that. I had my own money saved, not to mention the money and jewelry I took from Rich.

Downstairs we sat in the holding cell and they issued breakfast trays. I passed on it 'cause I knew I was getting out. There was no need in fuckin' up my appetite with bullshit-ass food. There were so many of us headed out that we took up three cells. Some were standing, but I secured my spot in the corner so I could doze off until we left. One thing I learned was these hos talked entirely too much. They would discuss their cases with anyone who would listen. I wasn't a regular when it came to being in the system, but I knew not to discuss my business. You never knew who was listening in order to get time shaved from their sentences.

It wasn't until seven when they opened the doors and started calling off names in alphabetical order. One-by-one they placed the shackles on the hands and feet of the women. All I could do was shake my head 'cause it seemed so inhumane. This was another process I couldn't get with: being caged like an animal.

"Kingston," the guard yelled. I stood up and walked into the hallway to get my restraints placed on. First she cuffed my hands, then my ankles. "Okay, go on over and get in line."

After they cuffed the last person, we were taken outside to the paddy wagon. I was sitting next to Mouth of the South, the one who wouldn't stop discussing her child abuse case on her boyfriend's child. Apparently the mother came and beat her ass right before she called the police on her ass. That served her right, but if it was me, I would've killed that ho and there would be no case. I would've been the judge and the jury.

"So, what you in here for?" She looked over at me.

I laughed and looked at the person next to me 'cause I know damn well she wasn't talking to me. "Who you talking to?" I asked.

"You. What you in here for?"

"And why is that your concern?"

"I was just asking a question." She frowned like I had offended her.

"Well, don't ask."

"Um. Excuse me."

"You excused. Just stay out of my business." I rolled my eyes and sat back in my seat in silence until we arrived at the courthouse and were placed in another holding cell.

Nine o'clock finally arrived, and I couldn't be happier when I was called out first. Shyne had put me up on game and warned me about the different runs. According to her, if my time was at eleven, I would be gone all day. It was best to be seen in the first batch.

When I walked into the courtroom I scanned the crowd, looking for my parents, Amon, and Mercedes. When I located them, my heart skipped a beat. I wanted to smile so badly, but I was more hurt than anything. Sitting next to Amon was Corey. Everything that happened between us resurfaced, and all I wanted to do was cry all over again. He hadn't been there in months, and out of the blue he was at my hearing. I already knew Mercedes or Amon was behind his presence.

We locked eyes for a long time, but neither one of us said a word or even made a gesture. Don't get me wrong, I was happy to see my support group in the stands, but a heads-up would've been nice. The day he left me was a day I would never forget. He walked away from me when I needed him the most. Could I blame him? No. Would I admit that to him? No.

I took my seat in front of them and faced forward. I couldn't force myself to turn around and face Corey once again.

We sat for fifteen minutes before the Judge stepped from her chambers.

"All rise. The Honorable Judge Sereni presiding." We all stood up.

"Thank you very much. Please be seated." The judge sat down and fumbled through some papers. "Today is September 20, 2017. Broward County Bond Court. I'm Judge Ella Sereni, the Chief Magistrate of Broward County. This is the case of the state versus Barbee Kingston. Ms. Kingston has been charged with one count of first degree murder and one count of robbery."

Just hearing my charges being read out in front of my parents made me cringe. This was not what I wanted them to hear, but I also knew they would find out eventually.

Tamela stood in front of the audience with confidence. There was no doubt in my mind I would walk out today. My mind never steered me wrong.

"Your honor, my client and I are filing a motion to have bail granted. Ms. Kingston has no criminal record, and she's a respected business owner, which means she's not a flight risk."

The D.A. interrupted my lawyer. "Your honor, her client has been charged with first degree murder and armed robbery. She's a threat to the community."

"Your honor, if you take a look at the evidence I have here, you will see my client was being held against her will by Richard Gathers, who is already in custody. Mr. Gathers also wrote a letter stating he accepts all charges and responsibility for the charges filed against my client." Tamela walked to the podium and passed the folder to the judge.

Judge Sereni opened the folder, then looked over in the direction of the prosecutor. "Did you receive this letter and speak to the attorney of Mr. Gathers?"

"Yes, we did receive it, your honor, but I don't think the defendant deserves to receive bail. She's dangerous, your honor."

"She's no more dangerous than Detective Rhines, who slapped my client during her interrogation," Tamela fired back.

"Is this true?" Judge Sereni had a slight scowl on her face.

"Yes, and it can be verified with Mr. Rhine's Boss, Lt. Taylor." Tamela wasn't playing games with the state.

"Okay, I need to see both of you in my chambers, now. We'll resume in 15 minutes. Court's in recess."

We all sat in silence while they exited the courtroom.

I could hear whispering behind me, but I couldn't stand to turn around and look Corey in the eyes again. He had a bitch hurting. I could admit I played a part in him leaving, but he didn't give me a chance to plead my case. That was a typical man, though. They could fuck up a million times and expect to be forgiven. Not women, though. We fuck up one time and it's over without a second thought.

Exactly fifteen minutes passed before the door opened and everyone returned. My lawyer's face was hard to read, so I wasn't sure if the news was good or bad. The judge looked in my direction and my heart skipped a beat.

"Ms. Kingston, after going through the files and statement from Richard Gathers, I am going to grant you bail. Your charges will remain and you will have to go to trial. You are not to engage in any type of illegal activity or get arrested. If you do, you will sit in the county jail until you are proven innocent or guilty. You are able to go to work and back home, nothing else. Do you understand that?"

"Yes, your honor." I didn't give a damn if she said I couldn't leave the house. I just needed to get the fuck up out of jail. This was no place for me.

"I'm going to set bail at one hundred thousand dollars. Court is adjourned." When she hit that gavel, I felt relieved. A wave of emotions took over my body and cleansed my soul like baptism water. Fresh tears built up in my eyes and trickled down my cheek. Just the thought of losing everything I worked for, my family, and never seeing the love of my life again made me weak in the knees. I stood up and hugged my attorney, holding on for dear life. I was far away from being free, but it was a start on clearing my name.

After court I couldn't wait to let Shyne know the good news. We had become quite close in such a short amount of time, and I confided in her about a lot of things, including the disappearance of Corey. Now, our friendship wasn't like the sisterhood I shared with Mercedes, but we were pretty damn close. And besides, I only told her things that weren't completely private.

When I walked into the dorm, Shyne was sitting at a table

watching T.V., so I walked over and tapped her shoulder. She looked up, smiling.

"What's up, baby girl? Did you get some good news?"

"You'll find out in a minute."

Shyne got up from the table and we walked back to her room. "So, the judge granted me bail." I dropped my hands down at my side.

"For real? That's good, B. I'm happy for you." She hugged me the same way I hugged my attorney in that courtroom. "Damn, you 'bouta leave a nigga already."

"Thanks, Shyne. I appreciate that."

She finally let me go, and there was a sadness in her eyes.

"Don't tell me you getting soft on me," I teased.

"Nah, just don't get out and forget about a nigga and shit." She laughed, but I knew she was serious.

"How can I forget about you?" I smiled back.

"That's what everybody say until they hit the door to freedom."

"Hell, I ain't been in here that long."

"I know."

"On the real, though, you can hit me up. I'll give you my number."

Shyne handed me a pen and a piece of paper. "I will be calling yo' ass, so don't act brand new and shit."

Shyne was real, and that's what I liked about her the most. "Nah, real nigga shit. I fuck with you."

Several hours later I was released and relieved to be out of those horrible living conditions. When I walked outside, I inhaled the fresh air. Being locked up made me appreciate the small things in life, such as bottled water and taking a shower without slides on.

As soon as I hit the corner, I paused. Corey and Mercedes

were outside waiting on me. I didn't know if I wanted to run and jump in his arms or slap his ass for all the shit he put me through. Whatever I decided, I needed to do it quick because I was getting closer by the second. The same butterflies he had always given me were fluttering around in my stomach like crazy.

I stopped within an arm's length of both of them.

"Girl, we missed you so much. These were the longest three weeks in history." Mercedes hugged me tight. "I never thought I would see you on the outside again."

"I know, right? I thought I was never getting out of there. Did you use my money to post my bond?" That was important 'cause I knew she had a tendency to not follow directions.

"That would be me." Corey grabbed my hand and pulled me close to him. "I couldn't stand to see you in there."

My mind said, *resist him*, but my body was saying, *bitch, are you crazy?* It felt good to be in his arms again, and I would be lying if I said I wasn't enjoying it.

"I missed you like crazy, B." His lips brushed up against my ear, and I swear my knees felt like they were about to give out at any moment.

"Yeah, I can tell." That was the quickest response I could give, and I also needed him to know I was upset with him. I pulled away from him. "Can we please get out of here? This place makes me sick."

We got into Corey's car and pulled out of the parking lot. "Are you hungry?" He glanced out of the corner of his eye.

"I'm too happy to eat right now. Take me straight home so I can shower."

"A'ight." He licked his lips, and lawd was that the sexiest shit I seen in weeks.

"So, did anybody try to take your virginity in there?" Mercedes joked.

76

"Girl, hell no. You know I don't play that shit. My roommate was a stud, but she was cool as fuck."

"She ain't never try you?"

"Hell nah, but this chick tried me in there over my roomie. I had to beat her ass and let her know these hands up-to-date."

After a twenty-minute ride of me telling them about my jail stint, we were finally pulling up in the parking lot. I couldn't wait to get inside and take a real shower.

"I'm going to go home, B. I'll catch up with you tomorrow." Mercedes hugged me once more.

"Why are you leaving?"

"You and Corey need to talk, and I want to give y'all some privacy. We have plenty of time to play catch-up."

"Okay, babes. I'll see you later." I closed the car door and headed toward the apartment in silence with Corey right behind me. I was praying Sierra was home because I wasn't ready to face Corey just yet.

The first thing I did was shower and fix me a glass of Patron. Corey was sitting down on the sofa, staring at the wall. Sierra wasn't there, so I knew this was about to be awkward. There was so much tension in the air that I didn't know where to begin. All I knew was I needed more time to think, because all of this was too sudden and unexpected. To ease my emotions, I downed the first glass and fixed another before I high-tailed it back to the bedroom to hide.

"We need to talk." Corey stopped me before I made it to the hallway.

"About what?"

"Everything."

"It's been a very long three weeks, and all I wanna do is relax and get my mind right."

Corey slid to the end of the couch. "We need to talk, for real."

"I don't want to. When you had the chance to talk to me, you left me. Remember? You didn't want to hear shit I had to say. You left me in the hospital, crying and screaming for you to stay with me."

Corey shook his head, and I could see the aggravation on his face. "I'm tellin' you to come and sit down so we can talk about it."

His tone was low, yet firm. I knew he was trying to demand some shit, but I didn't care. He wasn't worried about me when he was out doing whatever and whoever. "No. I don't want to," I reiterated.

"Sit cho ass down and listen to what I have to say!"

His bark caught my attention, and I knew he was serious. Corey never talked to me like that unless he was really mad at me. To prevent things from escalating any further, I walked over to the other couch and sipped slowly from my drink.

"Talk. I'm listening."

"The first thing you need to know is that my feelings for you never changed in my absence. I still love you, B. I've always loved you. Since we were younger."

"Then why did you leave me?"

"You slept with another man, and I couldn't handle that."

"But Cor –"

He held up his hand to cut me off. "Stop. Don't try to justify what you did. You was fuckin' me and that nigga at the same time. I read every single text message between y'all." Corey dropped his head. "You even fucked us in the same day, and you tried to insult my intelligence when I called you out on it."

"Corey, I'm sorry. I really am. I never thought about my actions or the consequences. Rich was only a pawn, and the plan was to only set him up. I never meant to sleep with him."

When he looked up, I could see the fire in his eyes. "And that's why you kept fuckin' him, huh? You must think I'm

78

some kinda fool to believe that shit."

"I had to. That was the only way to get close to him, and then onto Giovanni. It didn't mean anything. I swear it didn't." By this time tears were streaming down my face as he forced me to relive everything I did.

"That's bullshit."

"He kept me at a distance until I opened up to him. I never wanted to be with him. I only wanted you," I cried.

"Answer this question for me: how did you end up with him again?"

"He kidnapped me."

"Am I supposed to just take your word on that?"

"You saw the last messages he sent me. You saw what he did to me that night." I was an emotional wreck, and he wasn't making it any better.

"Why didn't you leave when Mercedes did?"

"He had a video of me in his phone robbing one of his targets. He said he would turn in the video if I didn't stay and help him."

"You seemed happy that night." Corey was acting as if I was lying to him, and it was breaking me down.

"Well, I wasn't," I screamed. "You don't know what I went through while I was there."

"Did you fuck him?"

I shook my head. "Corey, please don't do this."

"Did you fuck him?" he repeated himself, but I heard him the first time.

Answering that question would only push the dagger further into his heart, so I didn't respond.

"You can tell me the truth or I'm walking out for good this time, and I'll never come back. I promise you that."

I held my head down and cried harder. I loved Corey so much, and I just needed him to forgive me for everything I did.

When I finally got the nerve to leave Meat for good, I vowed to never love another man. After that failed relationship I just started playin' these niggas left and right, givin' no fucks about them. I did them the way they did females, but along came Corey, and he changed the game.

"I guess that means yes." Corey stood up and grabbed his keys.

"It was against my will," I blurted out.

I couldn't lose him. I loved him too much for that, and I knew he felt the same way because if he didn't, he would've never come to find me, let alone bail me out of jail.

"Rich raped me." I could hear his movement stop, so I looked up at him. I needed him to feel my pain. "He fucked me over and over again while I was tied up. Is that what you want to hear? And the whole time all I did was think of you and cry because there was nothing I could do to get away. I prayed every day that you would find me." I sniffled and wiped my tears with the back of my hand.

Corey walked over to me and I flinched, not knowing what to expect from him. After what I'd been through, I felt everyone was trying to hurt me.

"What you jumpin' for? I never put my hands on you."

"Rich did. He hurt me in more ways than you could ever imagine."

Sitting down beside me, Corey put his arms around me and held me tight. "Baby, I'm so sorry. I should've never left you like that. I had no idea what you went through."

"How could you? You didn't even ask." I cried in his arms and inhaled the scent of his cologne. This was all I ever wanted: to be loved by the man I would lay my life on the line for. "He hurt me bad, Corey."

"Don't worry, baby, that nigga gon' pay for what he did."

"He's in jail already. There's nothing you can do about that now. All I can do is move on."

"You'd be surprised at the type of reach I have. Trust me when I say this: that nigga gon' pay for this."

Destiny Skai

Chapter 7

Sierra

I was happy school was finally over. My entire day was spent thinking about Dre and the fact I was going to be a single teenage parent. What made matters even worst was my brother wanted to kill him, and I knew he was serious. All I could do was wait and see what happened next.

Before I unlocked the door, I took a deep breath. Corey was home, and I was hoping he didn't want to talk about it. I had enough to worry about, and the last thing I needed was for it to be rubbed in my face, as if I didn't feel bad enough about it.

When I stepped into the house, I was taken by surprise. On the couch were Corey and Barbee, and it looked like I had just interrupted something by the way they jumped. But I didn't care 'cause I was so happy to see her. I dropped my bag and ran to her.

"Sister, I missed you so much." I grabbed her arms and looked at her. "Are you okay?"

Barbee laughed and hugged me. "I'm fine, and I missed you, too." When she let me go, she placed her hand on my belly. "How's auntie's baby in there?"

"She's good." I cut my eyes at Corey. "We're good."

I was hoping he didn't tell B what was going on between me and Dre. That was something I wanted to do on my own. The last thing I wanted was for him to make it sound really bad. I needed her to hear my side of the story and how everything played out. The more I thought about it, the more it didn't make sense to me. Something happened to Dre, and I needed to know what it was. My mind wouldn't allow me to believe he would just up and abandon me without a valid reason. Corey could call me young and naïve, but I was far from crazy.

"You having a girl?" I guess she needed confirmation.

"Yes, we found out a few weeks ago."

"Is Dre happy, or did he want another boy?"

"Yeah, he was very happy." I choked up a bit and lost the words to say, but I needed to keep my composure. This wasn't about me. It was about my sister and the fact I missed her so much. My pain and emotional breakdown would have to wait until I was in my room alone, where I could cry in peace. I swear this baby turned me into a big-ass crybaby. Had me all emotional and in my feelings and shit. The old me would've went and beat Dre and Tokee's ass.

Barbee tilted her head to the side. "What do you mean?"

"Dre –"

Corey started to reply, but I interrupted him and gave him the side-eye. "It's a long story, but I'll tell you about it later."

Barbee nodded her head. "Okay, that's cool. I'm here whenever you ready."

"Are you out of jail for good?"

"I'm out on bail."

"Oh." That crushed my heart. I didn't want to lose her as a sister. "So, that means I could lose you?

Barbee grabbed my face. "I'm not going anywhere. I'll be right here to help you raise this beautiful baby girl you about to have."

"You promise?"

"I promise."

Corey stood up. "I'm about to head out. I guess I'll leave you two alone to play catch-up. Call me if y'all need me." He kissed us both on our cheeks and walked out the door.

When he left, I couldn't wait to fill her in on what went down. "There's so much that's been happening while you were away, and I had no one to talk to."

"Okay, sounds like I need a drink for this one." Barbee got

up and grabbed the bottle of Patron from the kitchen counter and came back to the couch. "Let's hear it."

"Okay, here goes." This conversation was about to be a poignant reminder of what I'd been through, so I pulled my feet underneath my thighs to get comfortable. There were a few pillows on the couch for decoration, so I picked one up and hugged it tight.

Five minutes into my heartfelt story, I was sobbing and crying into Barbee's arms. "You just don't understand what I've been going through, and Corey doesn't make it better. All he said was he told me this would happen. I just don't believe he would up and abandon me like that. He's been here for me all this time."

"When was the last time you tried to call him?"

"A few days ago I sent him a text, and he didn't respond." Barbee rubbed my back. "The last thing he told me was, whatever happened, not to doubt his love for me. It just doesn't sound right. I know something is wrong. Our last night together he poured his heart out to me and made love to me like he never did before."

Barbee lifted my head up. "Let's find out right now."

"I'm scared. What if – what if he's dead? Corey said he gon' kill him when he finds him."

"Let me go and find my phone. I'll be right back."

Barbee got up and went into the room. A few minutes later she returned with it and flopped down next to me on the sofa. "I'm going to call him right now."

She placed the phone on speaker and it just rang and rang.

"I told you."

Just as she was about to hang up, someone picked up.

"Who dis?" It was Dre.

Barbee put her hand over my mouth to keep me quiet.

Destiny Skai

Hearing his voice was a relief, but I didn't understand why he was ignoring my calls.

"Dre, this Barbee. What's up?"

"What's going on, B?"

"I'm trying to find out why you bailed out on Sierra like that? You didn't give her a warning or nothing. What's up with that?"

"B," he sighed heavily into the phone. "This shit deeper than rap right now. You wouldn't even understand."

"I'm listening." She rolled her neck and eyes as if he could see her.

"I can't discuss that right now, but in due time she'll find out why I did what I did."

Barbee jumped up from her seat as if they were face-to-face. Pointing her finger at the phone screen, she yelled into the phone, "Dre you gotta come on better than that. She's carrying your baby, and you got her stressed the fuck out. You trying to send her into labor early?"

"Her going into labor is the least of my worries."

Barbee frowned. "What the fuck you mean by that?" she snapped.

"It's not like that." He took a deep breath. "Listen, I love Sierra, but it's really complicated right now, and until I fix it, I can't see her."

Hearing him say he loved me sent a single tear streaming down my cheek. "Dre, I love you, too," I shouted. "I just don't understand why you doing this to me." My voice cracked as I tried to remind him my feelings hadn't changed even though he went ghost on my ass. I had thought this baby was gon' bring us closer, but it did the complete opposite, and I felt like a fool.

The phone was silent for a minute, and then the call ended.

When Dre hung up the phone, I cried for what seemed like hours. B did everything she could to get me to calm down, but

86

nothing could fix the dagger he shot through my heart. She managed to pull me from the couch and escort me into my bedroom. Curling up like I baby, I squeezed my pillow tight and buried my face in it.

My sister never left my side. That night she lay in bed with me while I cried myself to sleep.

***

Sierra

The next morning, on my way to school, Trina called me saying we should skip school, so I agreed. After I got off the bus, she was waiting on me in the loop.

"Come on, girl, let's go." She looked around to make sure campus security was nowhere in sight.

"Where are we going?" We walked quickly out of the gate and in the direction of the plaza.

"To chill with my boyfriend."

"Well, when did you get a boyfriend?"

"I met him a few weeks ago. I didn't say anything because I didn't know how things were going to work out between us." Trina smiled. "But everything seems like it's on the up-and-up, so it's all good."

"So, you got us cutting class for some new dick?" We posted up on the side of the building by the bus stop and waited.

"Girl, that dick ain't new. I been fuckin' that," Trina giggled. "That dick good, too."

"Yeah, I can tell, bitch. You got us skipping school for the dick."

Trina popped her mouth and shook her small hips. "I'll skip school for that dick. Get a zero, flunk out for that dick, I'll catch the bus for that dick. Bend it over, make it clap for that dick. I'll put my lips on that dick. Suck every single baby out that dick," she sang.

All I could do was laugh at her. No matter how bad I was feeling, she had the ability to change that. "Girl, shut up! I saw them dumb-ass videos on Facebook, and that shit getting on my nerves. They just keep coming up with these dumb-ass challenges."

"I don't see how, 'cause Dre had you doing all type of shit for that dick, too."

"Yeah, whatever." I sucked my teeth. "Where this nigga at?"

"He said he was on his way." Trina looked toward the traffic and pointed at a car. "I think that's him right there at the light."

A few seconds later a black Charger pulled up and rolled down the window. "It look like y'all need a ride," he grinned.

"Damn, took you long enough. Come on, bestie." We walked to the car and got in. "Stoney, this my best friend Sierra." Trina turned toward the backseat and looked at me. "Sierra, this Stoney."

"Nice to meet you, Sierra." Stoney pulled out of the parking lot and onto 44th street before making a right on University Drive.

"Same here."

I sat in the backseat and scrolled down my timeline on Facebook. A few people wrote "To Be Honest" posts on my wall. They were saying how fine I was and that I could dress.

It took us about 15 minutes before we pulled into a set of duplexes in Lauderhill. Stoney turned the car off and opened the door.

"Y'all, come on."

Trina jumped her li'l fast-ass out quick, but I moved just a little bit slower 'cause I wished I was with Dre instead.

Apparently she had been here before. This third-wheel shit was for the birds, and I wanted to be caked up with my own dick.

I followed behind them and Stoney let us in. "Have a seat on the couch. I'm about to get us something to smoke."

There was a dude sitting on a different sofa. He smiled when he saw us come in.

"What's up, Trina? Who is your friend?"

Trina placed her hand on my shoulder. "This my best friend, Sierra."

"Hey, best friend." The boy laughed, but I didn't see shit funny, and honestly I wasn't feeling the vibe.

"Hey." My response was dry as hell, but I didn't care. I needed him to understand ain't shit shaking over here.

He stood up and adjusted his gym shorts. "I'll be right back."

As soon as he disappeared into the room, I nudged Trina in the side. "Bitch, I ain't talking to his friend."

"Chill out. You don't have to." Trina and I sat down on the couch and waited on Stoney to come back. In the meantime, I told her about the call with Dre.

"Damn, that's crazy, Sierra. What kind of shit you think he into?"

"Girl, I don't know, but it sounds serious."

Trina sat up and smiled. "Girl, what if somebody wanna kidnap you or some shit?"

"Trina, I seriously doubt that. Why the hell would anyone wanna kidnap me?"

"You know drug dealers always have these arch nemeses, so they kidnap their girls for ransom and shit. You need to start watching the Investigation Discovery Channel, girl, 'cause you are clueless."

"No, you crazy, and even if that was the case, they could just kidnap his wife."

Trina always said she wanted to be a detective, and I told

her she should go for it. That girl was always trying to solve some shit with her nosey-ass.

Stoney and his friend came back into the living room. "I got some loud on deck. Y'all ready?" He sat down next to Trina and blazed the weed. Stoney took a few pulls, then passed it to her.

Trina must really trust this dude, 'cause she didn't see him roll up shit. But I guessed since they were fucking, she didn't need to see. She passed it to his homeboy.

"Best friend, you ain't smoking?" He was looking at me when he said that.

"Nah, I don't smoke. Thanks." And even if I did, I was told to roll my own shit. Dre taught me that.

After they were good and high, Trina and Stoney got up and went in the room. They weren't gone for a good five minutes before I heard loud moaning coming from the bedroom. That really had me uncomfortable. His friend kept looking at me like he wanted to fuck something.

"Why you so quiet?"

"'Cause I don't know you." I had a real attitude.

"We can change that. My name is Jay."

I nodded my head, but didn't say a word. Hopefully he would get the hint and leave me the fuck alone, because I wasn't interested in nothing he had to offer. Not even a conversation.

"Come sit next to me." He was patting the cushion next to him.

"I'm good. I'll stay right here."

"Damn, you mean, shorty."

"I'm not mean."

"I'm just trying to have some conversation with you, and you acting all crazy." Clearly he was annoyed.

"Listen, I have a man, and I'm not interested in talking."

"Whatever," he mumbled.

When Jay got up, I placed my hand on top of my bag because I was prepared to hit the big bitch with this stun gun. To my surprise, he kept walking to the front door. When he locked the door behind him, I knew he wasn't coming back. I was relieved and ready to go. The situation could've played out differently, and I was grateful it didn't. All Trina needed to do was get off the dick and have her dude drop me off. This was the last time I would come over here with her. I couldn't risk losing my baby behind something that could've been prevented.

The loud moaning and groaning was still going on, and now the headboard was screaming for dear life as it knocked hard against the wall. Trina's voice could be heard.

"Fuck me hard, zaddy. Ooh, right there. Ooh, yeah, beat this pussy up."

I could feel the seat of my panties getting wet. I squirmed in my seat because I was long overdue for some dick. My hormones were out of control and the one who was supposed to be feeding the baby had gone AWOL. It would probably have been the best time to invest in a vibrator, because what I wasn't about to do was let another man stick his dick inside of me. This pussy was on reserve until Dre got back. Whenever that was.

Thirty minutes later they finally came out of the room, and Trina was smiling from ear to ear. She was even walking funny. I was thinking, *damn, he doing it like that?*

"Where's Jay?" she asked.

I shrugged my shoulders. "Hell if I know. I'm ready to go, though. Barbee just called me, and I need to get home," I lied.

"We will after Stoney talks to us about getting some money." She sat down beside me and placed her feet on the couch.

One of Stoney's brows shifted. "Barbee?" he repeated. "You mean Blacque Barbee?"

"Yeah. Why?"

"Oh, nothing. I know her from back in the day, that's all. That's your sister?"

"Yeah." I wasn't sure what he was getting at, but I didn't like to be questioned.

"Okay. So check this out, Sierra." Trina placed her hand on my knee. "We have an opportunity to make some money, and Stoney is going to help us."

I had to stop her right there. "I ain't selling no pussy."

Stoney laughed. "I ain't no pimp, baby girl."

"So, what you talking about, then?"

Stoney leaned forward with his hands folded in front of him. "This all you gotta do."

For ten minutes Stoney tried to convince me a hundred different ways why I should come and work for him. The shit he wanted us to do sounded crazy as fuck. Robbing dope boys was not a hustle I was interested in, and I couldn't understand how Trina thought this was a good idea. This nigga clearly had her brainwashed and dick-whipped. One thing I knew: Sierra wasn't doing it. I wasn't hurting for money, and anything I needed, Corey would get it for me.

"Nah, I ain't on that. I'll pass."

"Think about it, Sierra. You have a baby on the way, and you don't know what's going on with Dre. For all you know, he may never come back."

"No, Trina. I'm not doing it. Can you please just take me home?"

Stoney stood up. "Yeah, I can do that, but I want you to think about it."

"There's nothing to think about. I'm not doing it."

Stoney laughed and rubbed his hands together. "Well, think about this." He paused and rubbed the hair on his chin. "What you think your sister did for a living? Her and her best friend, Nehiya, used to run with my uncle Fox back in the day. Setting niggas up and shit. As a matter of fact, I just saw her a few months back in Jacksonville with some nigga. So yeah, she back to her old tricks once again."

Listening to Stoney talk about Barbee like that had my mind racing. If he was telling the truth, then that would explain a lot of the things that went on. The shooting, her kidnapping and arrest. Maybe Barbee wasn't the saint I painted her out to be. Deep down I just wanted to cry, but most importantly I wanted the truth.

"I don't believe you."

"How do you think she lives so lavishly? It ain't the nigga she with. Barbee been getting money since she was sixteen. The same age as you. The only difference is she was pushing a Lexus when all the young chicks was catching rides and buses. She a true hustler."

I was sure the expression on my face disclosed the fact I was clueless about her lifestyle. My body sunk into the seat because this was a lot to take in about the woman I idolized so much.

Stoney placed his hand on my shoulder. "I know it's a lot to take in at once, but I'm going to leave you with something to back up what I said. Go to your Google search engine and type in Barbee's name. Then I want you to type in 'The Fox Hotel murder.' You'll see the article on my uncle."

My fingers shook as I typed the information into my search bar. I watch closely as my screen loaded. Moments later everything Stoney told me was right there in my face, clear as the daylight outside. I read every article, and for the first time I felt betrayed by Barbee. A few tears pricked the back of my eyes, but I wouldn't allow them to fall. I needed to cry in private.

I placed my phone back into my bag and looked Stoney in the eyes. "I'll sleep on it and let you know tomorrow.

Chapter 8

Dre

The past few weeks away from Sierra had me fucked up. My baby stayed on my mind 24/7. If I had it my way we would be together, but due to my situation I had to let her go. After I dropped her off at school that morning, I went home and straightened Tokee about telling her uncle my muthafuckin' business. Since then I'd been staying at the crib. I could no longer call it a home. I'd also been sleeping in the room with my son 'cause fuckin' Tokee was not something I wanted to do. Every day I spent in that house was a constant reminder I should've never married her in the first place. I should've handled that money situation out the gate and none of this would be happening.

My main focus was to get this money and make sure all of my ducks was in a row. So, that's exactly what I did.

I pulled up on my first pick-up, Pete in Franklin Park. He was sitting on a bench, shooting the shit wit' an old coon when I walked up on him.

"Where the fuck you been at, my nigga?" We dapped it up.

"Hustlin'. You got that cash for me?"

"Yeah, it's in the whip."

"Well, let's grab that shit, 'cause I got moves to make." It was hotter than a muthafucka out the door, and I wasn't tryin' to sit out in the sun wit' that nigga. We walked across the street to where his Cutlass was parked on the curb. He popped the trunk.

"Aye, yo, Corey slid up on me the other day lookin' for you."

I already knew what it was about. "What he said?"

"If we see you, deliver the message that he lookin' for you."

Pete passed me an envelope, so I slipped it into my pocket

without counting it. That would be done once I got in the car. I wasn't worried, but I needed to be sure. Money would make a nigga switch on his closest partna.

"A'ight, I'm outta here. I'll catch up wit' cha later."

"Aye, check this out, though." Pete checked his surroundings and rubbed his nose with his thumb before he continued. "Slide light, 'cause I heard that nigga got a bounty on ya head for ten racks."

I nodded my head 'cause I didn't think the shit was that deep, but I underestimated him. "Bet that up."

"Be safe, my nigga."

I walked off.

If it wasn't one thing, it was another. First the shit with Louie, and then the beef with Corey. I swear a nigga couldn't win for losing, but this shit was my fault, though. Now I had a target on my back, so I had to really keep my ears and eyes open. A man's closest niggas will do his ass in for them racks. One thing for certain, and two thangs fa' sho. I wasn't goin' out like no bitch, though. Whoever ran up on me was gettin' wet with no hesitation.

A few hours passed and I was finally done making all of the pick-ups from the other niggas who owed Louie from the shipment. The day after I left Sierra, I stepped to him and let him know she was gone for good. All was forgiven, and we were able to move on with business as usual.

The liquor store was calling my name, so I slid up to J&L on 19th Street and got me a fifth of Remy. It wasn't gon' make my problems go away, but it would numb me for a while. I sat in the car and fixed myself a drink before I took off. Riding around and drinking wasn't safe for me, but that's how bad I didn't wanna go back to the crib. During these times I would normally call Sierra, and we would hang out at different times of the night. She was always my voice of reason and that comfort a nigga needed. Sierra had her ways, but she knew how to stay in her place. She preferred to be her man's medicine and not his headache. Tokee, on the other hand, did not know how to decipher between the two, and that's what pushed me into the arms of another woman. A younger woman, at that.

I rode around the city for about an hour before I decided to take it in. I pulled up into my driveway and took a deep breath. Lord knows I didn't want to go in there. I punched the steering wheel. My life was fucked up right now, and I needed to fix it fast. Time was dwindling away. Pulling out my cellphone, I opened up the slew of texts from Sierra. Her last text a few days ago was what hurt me the most.

The baby is constantly moving and this is supposed to be the happiest time of my pregnancy, but instead I'm depressed. I can't sleep or eat cause you just abandoned us like we don't mean nothing to you. I wish you were here to rub my stomach and calm her down ☹ I love you Dre and I wish u loved me too. I will never call u again. Goodbye.

I played the song *Exchange* and reminisced on our last night together while I reread her message over and over again. Smoking anything other than weed was a no for me, but that night I bought a Black n' Mild and fired it up. The Remy really had me in my feelings. I took a few puffs and turned the bottle of Remy up to my lips. The sips from the cup was taking too long to get me where I needed to be before I walked into the lion's den.

Thirty minutes had passed, and I was still sitting there listening to that song on repeat. I had even shed a few tears, and I never cried over a female before. That's how I knew me and her were meant to be.

It was time to go in the house, so I turned the car off and got out. I took one step forward and I felt a piece of steel on the back of my head. I was drunk, but not so drunk I didn't know it was a banger. Whoever it was had to be waiting on me to come home.

"Fuck-nigga, you got any last words for my sister before I color your driveway with your blood?"

I guess Corey decided to do his own dirty work. "You been following me, huh? I heard about the tag on my head."

"I know those ain't ya last words."

"'I love your sister are my last words, but I think you should hear me out before you pull that trigger."

"What the fuck I need to listen to you for? I warned you about my sister, and you fucked her over anyway. So, before I let you hurt her more than you already did, I might as well put the nail in ya coffin."

"If you kill me, she'll never forgive you."

"I wouldn't be so sure about that."

"I talked to her the other day. You might wanna rethink this." He pulled the hammer back, and I knew what was next. "Corey, hear me out before you do that, please. The only reason I left your sister is because Louie told me to."

"What the fuck he gotta do with this?" Corey pressed the barrel deeper into my scalp.

"A few months back I was robbed for Louie's shipment worth 500K. I ain't have that kind of cash to replace it, so to clear my debt I had to marry Tokee. I didn't want to, but I didn't have a choice. So, a few weeks ago he confronted me about my new chick and baby on the way. He showed me a picture of Sierra and said he had a shooter at her school to take her out if I didn't cooperate. I couldn't do shit 'cause I was at the house with the nigga. I had to leave her."

"Nigga, you think I believe that shit?"

"I can show you, but I need to pull out my phone."

98

"Do it slow or I'll blast you right now."

I reached into my pocket and pulled out the phone. Once I had the message box open, I held the phone out so he could see for himself.

"Where this nigga at?" Corey asked.

"I got it under control. I have a plan to take this nigga out and get rid of Tokee for good."

"Nah, I want in 'cause this nigga got me fucked up 'bout my sister. Just like you."

"Corey, you know me, man. And you know fuckin' well I ain't gon' abandon my responsibilities like that. I took care of her while you was gone."

Corey didn't say anything, but I could feel him move the banger. "You got one week or the next time you see me it's lights out."

He walked away, and I went inside the house. The plan I had for Louie had to happen quicker than I originally orchestrated.

***

Sierra

After hearing what Stoney had to say about Barbee, I was still in disbelief. So, when I got home I continued with my research. I searched google for an hour trying to dig up anything on her case I could find. The charges she was facing were murder and armed robbery. Now that made me wonder if that was the reason Corey left her in the first place. The article also stated she had an accomplice named Richard. That must be the dude Stoney was talking about.

Knock! Knock!

Corey wasn't home yet, so I knew it was B. With how I was

feeling right then, I couldn't force myself to talk to her. I was just so disappointed in her. And maybe I didn't have a reason to be, but that's how I felt. Everything around this house was done discreetly, and they treated me like I was a damn child. No one cared to fill me in on nothing. I was always left in the damn dark.

One day I would ask her about it, but tonight wasn't it. I pretended to be asleep so she would go away.

While I stared up at the ceiling, I heard the front door open and then some movement. Then I heard Corey ask where I was. It was late, and the first thing on my mind was *did he do something to Dre?* I got up slowly and stood next to the door with my ear pressed against it.

"Is she asleep?" he asked.

"I think so. I knocked on her door not too long ago and she didn't answer," B replied.

"We gotta talk."

"What happened?"

"Let's go in the room."

I waited until I heard the door close before I snuck out of my room. Quietly, I placed my ear as close as I could get it to the door without making a sound.

"I caught Dre slippin' tonight."

As soon as he said that, my heart skipped several beats and I wanted to pass out right then and there.

"Baby, you killed him?" B asked.

"Nah. I caught the nigga at his house, so I snuck up on him and put that heat to the back of his head. The nigga knew it was me." I was so relieved when he said that. "So, the nigga tells me the reason he dipped out on Sierra is 'cause Tokee uncle Louie told him to."

"What do you mean, he told him to?"

"He knows Sierra is pregnant from Dre and he was cheating

on Tokee. He showed him a picture of Sierra and said he had a shooter at the school ready to take her down."

"Hold up!" Barbee snapped. "How the fuck he gon' tell him to leave her alone? And how he think he gon' get away with a threat like that? We need to go and see this nigga." I could hear the hostility in her voice.

"Calm down Bonnie," Corey laughed. "We got this shit under control. Dre said he have a plan in motion, but I told the nigga he had a week to get at me. And if he don't, the next time he see me he won't get a chance to explain 'cause I'ma bust his shit wide open."

"Okay, one week it is. If not, we goin' to see 'bout that nigga. Simple as that."

"Damn right. That's why I fucks with you like that. You my gangsta-ass bitch."

"You goddamn right. Now fuck me like you missed me."

I had to get the fuck away from the door quickly 'cause my ears heard just a little too much. They were beyond nasty. And clearly her murder rap wasn't an issue for him or the reason he left. Maybe he liked that shit after all.

Once I was in my room, I closed and locked the door before crawling into bed. A few minutes had passed, and I could hear slight moaning. I wasn't on this shit night, and if I heard one more person fuckin' and it wasn't me, I was gon' lose it. To put an end to that problem, I put my earphones in and fell asleep to me and Dre's favorite song.

That night I slept like a baby. I felt a whole lot better knowing Dre didn't jump ship. Within a week everything would be back to normal, and my man would be in my arms and finally between these legs. My coochie needed some serious TLC, and no one could do it better than him. I swear the sound of anything sexual or similar had me ready to bust a nut at any given moment.

Corey and Barbee must've had a long night because neither one of them was awake when I left for school that morning. After hearing that news, I couldn't force myself to go to school. All I kept thinking about was if I went today, would it be my last day alive? After careful consideration I chose to ditch school and hit up Trina to see where she was.

"Hey, bestie!"

"You sound like you having fun over there." I walked through the parking lot slowly.

"Yeah, I'm just chillin', you know? What's going on?"

"It don't sound like you going to school today."

"Nah, I'm with my baby today, so I'm gon' need your homework later."

"Who said I was going to school?" I stood out front at the bus stop.

"Oh, excuse me. I thought you were."

"Not today. I'm trying to see what Stoney talkin' about. I want in on that."

"What changed your mind?"

"I did a lot of thinking, and I need to be able to take care of my baby when she gets here."

"Okay, so you about to come through?"

"How, girl? I ain't got no car, and you know I need a ride."

"Okay, but you gon' have to meet us."

"Where?"

"Hold on, let me check." I could hear muffled noises like she was moving around and talking at the same time. After a few seconds it came to an end. "He said be in front of the school."

"Okay, bye, 'cause the bus here."

"Yeah."

The school bus stopped in front of me, and I got on and

102

went straight to my seat in the middle. I sat solo 'cause I didn't want to be bothered. On the way to school my attention was focused on Facebook. I created a post that said "Time to chase this schmoney!!!"

Back at Stoney's place, we sat together and discussed our game plan for the night.

"You nervous?" he asked.

I shrugged my shoulders. "A little bit."

"Don't worry, we'll be right there with you. All you gotta do is get inside, and I'll do the rest."

Stoney rubbed my shoulders and sent an awkward chill over my body. It was uncomfortable, to say the least. There was something about his touch that made me feel uneasy. "Okay," I agreed.

Trina was just sitting there with this blank expression on her face. Something was clearly going on between the two of them, but I didn't want no part of it. All I wanted to do was get my money and call it a day.

A few hours had passed, and the darkness was bestowed upon us. "Y'all ready?" Stoney was wearing jack-boy clothes, for certain. That all-black was a dead giveaway to anybody in the hood.

"As ready as I'm gon' be." My nerves were shot to hell, and we hadn't even got in the car yet. A bitch had the shakes and shit.

"Hell yeah." Trina jumped up and down, wielding a gun in her hand.

"Yo, put that shit down before you shoot one of us." Stoney snatched the gun from her hand. "Always remember guns don't kill people, but stupid people with guns do."

Trina's attitude changed quickly, and she was no longer in that happy mood. She sat down and didn't say another word.

Stoney placed the guns inside of a book bag and threw it over his shoulder. "Let's ride."

It took us 15 minutes to get to Dillard, and I sat in the backseat sweating like a rotisserie chicken in the oven the entire ride. We hit Fifteenth Street and passed some duplexes.

"That's the spot right there, Sierra. And you see that nigga on the porch?" He glanced at me in the rearview mirror. I nodded my head yes. "That's the nigga who own the trap, so that's who you want."

"Got it."

Stoney drove me to the end of the street and I got out. I swear I had never been so nervous in my life, but I knew I needed to do this in order to complete my mission, so I took a few deep breaths in an effort to slow down the pace of my heart. But hell, walking up the street was about to be a task within itself.

My bare feet hit the pavement, and it did not feel good whatsoever. Sand was in between my toes and I stepped on a damn pebble. "Shit," I mumbled. The sidewalk wasn't getting it, so I took it to the street. That didn't make the walk any better, but at least I wouldn't have to worry about no more pebbles.

It probably took me a good five minutes to get close to his house. I would've gotten there sooner, but my feet were hurting. That's when I went into my acting mode. I crossed back over to the sidewalk to make sure I was close enough. I dialed Stoney's number and put my phone up to my ear.

"How could you do this to me?" I cried into the phone. Tears were something I was able to produce quickly. Fuckin' with Dre, I could shed them bitches at the drop of a dime. Maybe I could be an actress, especially after the performance I was about to give.

"So you would really put me out the car in this dangerous-ass neighborhood to walk while I'm pregnant with your child?"

As I walked past, I could see him looking at me from the corner of my eye.

"Tony, I don't have on any shoes, and I have no money to get home. What the fuck is wrong with you?" I didn't scream, but I spoke loud enough for him to hear me. Dropping the phone to my side, I fell to my knees and cried harder.

Not even a minute later, I felt a hand touch my shoulder. "Hey, ma, are you okay?"

I looked up at him with sadness in my eyes. "No. My baby daddy just left me here, stranded. I don't have on any shoes or money to get home.

He lifted me by the arm. "Get up, ma. You don't need to be going through all of that. Where do you live?"

"Hollywood," I lied. I knew if I told him I lived closer, he would try to give me a ride. This dude appeared to be young, but these days I could never tell 'cause black don't crack.

"I can pay for an Uber so you can get home safe."

When he smiled at me, I smiled back. He was a real piece of eye candy with that beautiful smile and well-groomed dreads. I had a thing for chocolate men, and he was looking mighty delicious. "You would do that for me?" I leaned forward and brushed the sand from my knees.

"I have sisters, and I would want someone to do the same for mine if it were to happen to them." He looked around and checked his surroundings. "You can come inside and wait if you want to."

I rocked side-to-side as if I was in deep thought. "I don't know if that's a good idea."

"Listen, ma, I'm not gon' do anything to you. I promise." He held his hand out for me to grab. "Trust me."

In my head I was saying, *You shouldn't trust me.* I placed my hand into his and allowed him to lead the way inside the apartment.

"Here, have a seat. And I'm Bo, by the way." He pointed to a spot on the sofa, so I took a seat and sat my phone face-down.

"Nice to meet you, Bo." My hands were in my lap, and I was hoping he didn't sense my nervousness.

"Normally when people introduce themselves, the other person gives their name, too," Bo laughed.

"Sorry. I'm Mona." I was too busy looking around and observing the tidiness of a real, live trap-house. The kitchen was right where the living room was, so I could see the other with no problems. The entertainment system was dope as fuck. He had a built-in fish tank at the bottom and big-ass TV at the top.

"You want something to drink?" Bo opened up the fridge. "I have bottled water and Gatorade."

"Water would be fine, thanks."

When he handed me the bottle and walked to the back room, I picked up my cellphone to see Stoney was still on the line, listening. "I'm ready," I whispered and hung up quickly before he returned to the room.

Bo had a pair of sandals in his hand. "Here, put these on. I bought 'em for my girl, but I'll get her another pair."

"Thank you." I took them out of his hand and slipped my feet into them. They were a perfect fit, and to top it all off, they matched my Tory Burch bag perfectly.

Five minutes later there was a knock on the door and my heart began to race. *Showtime,* I thought. I swallowed the saliva that dripped inside my mouth. I could feel myself wanting to throw up. The baby started to move, so I put my hand on my belly and rubbed my baby girl to calm her down.

Bo approached the door. "Who is it?" He put his eye to the peephole. "Who is it?" he repeated. There was no answer.

Bo stooped down by the sofa and pulled out a gun. Now I was really scared. He unlocked the door and pushed it open, gripping his ratchet in his hand. I guess he didn't see anybody.

Just as he was closing the door, someone snatched it open, knocking him off balance.

"Not so fast." Stoney placed his Nina in Bo's face and stepped inside. "Drop that shit."

Trina came in behind him and closed the door. They both had on black masks with the eyes cut out.

Bo dropped the ratchet and backed up. "Ain't this about a bitch."

"Ah!" I screamed and covered my mouth.

"Shut the fuck up, bitch, before I blast yo' ass," Stoney spat. "Where the shit at?" he pushed Bo.

"It's in the room, man. Just leave the girl alone."

"Fuck that bitch." Stoney looked back at Trina. "Don't let that bitch out your sight."

She walked in front of the couch and aimed her gun at me. That shit made me uncomfortable as fuck. The last thing I needed was a freak accident.

When they disappeared into the room, Trina lowered her weapon. "Bitch, you look scared," she whispered, trying to keep herself from laughing.

"Yeah, 'cause you pointing that shit at me." My voice was low as well. The last thing I needed him to hear was us having a conversation.

Trina waved it around. "Chi', this thing ain't loaded. I don't even know how to aim a gun, let alone shoot one."

Stoney could be heard from the other room telling Bo to hurry up and pack up the shit. I was hoping they didn't kill him because he seemed like a really good dude.

Trina came closer to me. "Listen, when I walk in the room, I want you to open and close the door real hard, and then be still."

"Okay."

When Trina walked away, I eased to the door and waited for her to step inside. As soon as she did, I slammed the door hard and stood in the middle of the living room.

"Who the fuck is that?" Stoney yelled.

Trina stepped out into the hallway. "That bitch ran."

"Go catch the bitch."

"Nah, man, just let her go. She ain't gon' say nothing. Bae, tie this nigga up and let's go." Trina was trying to get up out of there.

"A'ight, let's do it."

It took them about five minutes to tie him up before they came out to where I was. Stoney nodded his head toward me and we hit the front door quick. Hearing Bo plead for my life made me feel bad for what I was doing, but I needed my man back more than anything in this world. At least Bo was alive, and he could always make his money back. And sooner rather than later I would have to check my feelings at the door if I wanted to become a real jack-girl.

Chapter 9

Barbee

Over the last few days Sierra had been coming in the house later than usual, and there was a drastic change in her behavior. I couldn't put my finger on it because, for one, she was already pregnant, so that meant she didn't change for some dick. It was something else, and I was going to figure that shit out soon. I remembered going through the same changes when I was with Meat and Fox.

The school also called and said she missed a few days of school. That was unlike her, and if I didn't know anything else, I knew her education was important to her. Every morning she left ready for school, and that made me wonder what she really had going on, the company she was keeping, and what she was doing.

I sat on the sofa and waited on her to come out. Corey was in the bed asleep, and I didn't want to wake him up, being that I could handle this on my own. We had a great relationship, so I figured it would be best not to involve him at the moment.

Sierra's bedroom door opened and she stepped out with her bag slung across her back. She had a slight frown on her face as she approached me.

"Good morning, sunshine," I smiled.

"Good morning." Her tone definitely didn't match mine, so I sensed she wasn't in a good mood. But hell, maybe it was her hormones acting up.

"The school called and said you missed a week. What's going on with you?"

Sierra stopped in her tracks. "Snitches," she mumbled under her breath, but I heard her loud and clear.

"Why haven't you been to school? You know if you miss

too many days, they can kick you out."

"It hasn't been that many, and I'm about to head there now."

I rubbed my hands together. "You've never lied to me before, so let's not start that now."

Sierra folded her arms and rolled her eyes. "Too bad I can't say the same thing about you."

Now she had my attention. I stood up and placed my hands on my hips. "And what is that supposed to mean?"

"Why did you go to jail? What did you do?" She looked me in my eyes and didn't bat a lash

"That's a question I don't have to answer. That's on a need-to-know basis, and you don't need to know that. All I will say is I'm innocent, and I didn't do what they claim I did."

"If you say so." Sierra flipped her hair and walked off. "I'm about to miss my bus. I'll see you later."

If it wasn't for Corey and the good Lord holding my tongue, I would've got her ass right together, but I let her have that. Instead I went outside to see if she was really getting on the bus. Stepping onto the porch, I closed the door behind me and headed toward the parking lot. I would've thought that after the kidnapping I would keep the damn door locked, but it was okay 'cause Corey was in there.

To keep myself from being seen, I didn't cut across the parking lot. I walked on the sidewalk at a fast pace. Once I had her in my eyesight, I slowed down. The bus hadn't arrived yet 'cause I could see all the students waiting by the entrance. There was a bench in the cut next to some trees, so I sat down and waited.

About five minutes later the big cheese was finally pulling up, so I got up to go back to the house. I walked slowly and kept my eyes on her to make sure she got on. After the last student got on, Sierra walked away from the bus, so I headed in her direction. The bus driver looked like she was saying something to her before she closed the door and pulled off.

I started to jog toward her. Just then a car pulled up and came inside the entrance. I knew it was for her, but I knew it wasn't Dre.

Sierra opened the passenger door and got in, and just as she was closing the door I was right up on her.

"So, you lied again? I thought you was going to school."

"I am going. I'm just not taking the bus."

Placing my hand on the door, I pushed it open. "Nah, get out the car. I'm not letting you go nowhere."

"B, chill. My friend is giving me a ride to school."

Not once did I think to see who the driver was, but when I leaned down and saw a familiar face, my chest began to tighten and breathing picked up. Never in a million years did I think the two of them would ever cross paths.

"Stoney!" I shouted.

He looked up at me and grinned. "What's good, Blacque Barbee? I never thought I would run into you like this."

"Sierra, get out the car."

"For what? I didn't even do nothing."

"Get out the car now." All I knew was I couldn't let her leave with him. Stoney picked up where Fox left off, and I already knew what type of relationship these two were trying to build. It would explain why she'd been acting that way.

"Blacque Barbee, chill, baby. I ain't gon' do nothing she don't want me to do."

"Nah, I can't have her hangin' with you. I already know how you play." I tried to pull her arm, but she snatched away from me.

"B, stop trippin', cause I'm not gettin' out. I know all about you and how you get money. Stoney told me." She shook her head. "And all this time I looked up to you, not knowing that this the type of lifestyle you live."

"Sierra, you don't know nothing about my lifestyle or why I did any of the shit I did. You have it made right now, and you don't need to get involved. The streets ain't no place for a little girl that think she know what's going on."

"Yeah, whatever." She turned and looked at Stoney. "Pull off so we can get this money."

I wasn't no fool, so I stepped out of the way and let him drive off. If I had my gun, I would've put a slug between that fuck-nigga's eyes. If Sierra only knew the danger she just put her and that baby in, she would've got out the car. At that moment there was nothing I could do, so I walked back to the apartment to wake up Corey. Maybe he could talk some sense into that crazy-ass girl. My gut served me right, though. I knew there was a new person in the equation because she just up and changed out of the blue. However, it was worse than I thought it was. I would rather she been in the car with any other nigga walking instead of Stoney. That nigga was nasty, and he slept with all his female workers.

As soon as I made it back inside, I went into the room to get Corey, but he was already up.

"We have a problem." I stood in front of him with my hands on my hips.

"And what's that?" He looked up through hooded eyes. I could tell he was ready to be on the defense, but little did he know this was not about us.

"It's Sierra."

"What about her?"

"She's been skipping school, so I confronted her about it."

"When were you gon' tell me about it?"

"Well, I wanted to talk to her first and see what was going on before I brought you into it."

"I'm her guardian. I'm supposed to be into it."

This nigga loved to remind me he was in charge of

112

everything, but now wasn't the time. My eyes rolled slightly before I responded. "Anyway, I confronted her about it she said it was nothing and she was going to school today. So I followed her outside and she was getting in the car with some nigga. I get to the car and it was Stoney."

Corey's upper lip curled. "Who the fuck is Stoney?"

"Fox's nephew. The nigga I used to run with back in the day."

"Hell nah, she ain't with that nigga."

"I told her to get out the car, but she wouldn't. And the fucked-up part about it is he told her everything about me."

Corey leaned over and picked up his cellphone off the nightstand. "I'm about to call her."

"She probably not gon' answer, Corey. There was something in her eyes I never seen before."

He dialed her number, but she didn't pick up. He tried two more times and still nothing. He sat the phone down and took a deep breath. "We gotta find my sister."

***

Sierra

A few days had passed and I still hadn't been home yet. Me, Stoney, and Trina had been staying at a motel getting this money. So far we took down four trap houses and came across some major bread. Barbee and Corey has been blowing my phone up, but I'd been dodging their calls. I already knew what the deal would be when I got back, so I was preparing to be on my own after.

To be honest, I never wanted to disrespect Barbee because she had been so good to me. The problem I had with her is she lied to me, and so did Corey about what had been going on all this time. Her way of living brought on all the heartache and pain she endured from her sisters' deaths and even their unborn child.

It hurt to know someone I looked up to wasn't living right in the first place, but giving out advice.

"Aye, Sierra, you wanna hit this?" Stoney was coughing and holding the blunt in between his fingers.

"You know damn well I can't smoke." I was sitting on the bed and Trina was across from me in the chair.

"Shit, I know crackheads that had healthy babies. And besides, it's just weed. It ain't gon' do shit."

Trina reached for the blunt. "Gimme the weed. Shit, I ain't pregnant." She took one too many pulls and started choking. "This shit 'bouta kill me."

While they got high and drunk, I sat there listening to music and thinking about Dre, as usual. I just wanted this whole thing to be over with 'cause I was tired of being away from him.

Stoney stood up, walked over to where I was sitting, and stood in front of me. I leaned back a little bit because I was unaware of what he was about to do. He was lit, so who knew. "Why you standing in front of me like that?"

"You scared of me?"

"What I'ma be scared of you for?"

Stoney grabbed his dick and shook it. "You scared of this, though?" He licked his lips.

I didn't know what was wrong with him, but he had the wrong girl. I only slept with one man in my life, and that was Dre, and that's the way I planned on keeping it. Fear filled my heart 'cause I had never been in such a compromising situation before. I looked over at Trina.

"Can you get your man, please?"

"He straight." She looked away and sipped her drink.

Stoney raised his arm and used his finger to outline my

nipple. "You got some nice titties. You wanna breastfeed me?"

He laughed, but I didn't see the humor in it. Instead, I slapped his hand away and shielded my chest with my arms. "Stop touching me."

"If you want this money you will let me touch on whatever I want."

My heart sank to the pit of my stomach. I couldn't believe what was happening to me, and the bitch who was supposed to be my best friend was sitting there like a fuckin' mute. The only reason I was in that sleazy-ass hotel and pulling capers was for the money. "That wasn't part of the deal. I set them niggas up, just like you asked me to."

He unbuckled his pants. "No pussy, no money. It's simple as that. So think about it while I get my dick sucked."

Stoney dropped his pants and his boxers before he turned away and walked over to Trina. She immediately got on her knees and sucked him up. There was no way in hell I would be doing that. I couldn't understand if he was supposed to be her man, then why was he trying to fuck me? And why was he making her suck his dick in front of me? Dre would've never tried me like that.

For the next ten minutes all I heard was a slurping sound and him grunting every now and again. That shit really turned my stomach. Stoney had her by the hair, fucking her mouth.

"Shit," he moaned, snatching his piece from the grip of her lips. "That's enough. I can't nut yet."

Trina got up from the floor and sat back down in the chair. She had a frown on her face. Stoney walked toward me, stroking his dick in one hand. "You ready for me?"

I tried to stand up, but he pushed me onto the bed. "I don't wanna get aggressive with you 'cause you pregnant, so come out them clothes and let's get this over with."

"Come on, please don't do this," I begged.

"Sierra, just do it," Trina shouted.

"Why would I wanna fuck your boyfriend?"

He tossed his head back and burst out into laughter. "Boyfriend? I'm not her boyfriend. All we do is smoke, fuck, and get money. Nothing more, nothing less. If she was my girlfriend, you think I would be trying to fuck you, too? Think of me as a pimp, in a way. Without the prostitution, of course."

Stoney grabbed my pants and tried to unfasten them, but I grabbed the top of them to stop him. "I'm not doing this."

He looked over his shoulder at Trina, who was in a daze. "Gimme my gun."

"Okay, okay, please don't. I'll do it," I cried. "Just please wear a condom. Please."

I released the hold I had on the button and took a deep breath. Slipping from my pants, I kicked them onto the floor and scooted to the middle of the bed. This was not what I had planned, and just the thought of having another man inside me besides Dre felt like the ultimate betrayal. I closed my eyes and said a silent prayer in hopes that this torture would be over quickly.

Stoney slipped a condom on his dick and climbed on top of me. "I wanted to fuck you the first time I saw yo' fine ass."

The sound of his voice was making my skin crawl, and I just wanted to run up outta there. Forcing his dick inside of me, I held my breath and turned my head to the side. Hopefully the head he received would shorten his time. Stoney pushed in and out of me, and I hated every minute of it. His dick was big, but there was no desire for me, so quite naturally I was dry.

"Open your legs up for me." He leaned down, spit on his dick, and rubbed my clit. "I need this pussy wet."

The whole time he thrust in and out of me, I just lay there and cried. I had never been raped before or taken advantage of, and I didn't have the best upbringing. Although I lived in a

116

group home, I remained safe at all times.

Tears were rolling down the sides of my face as I breathed heavily. The sweat from his face dripped onto mine, but I didn't bother to wipe it off. I caught a glimpse of Trina, and she was just sitting there looking dumb while she played on her phone. When this was all over, I had something for that bitch for letting this go down.

"Damn, pregnant pussy so good. Shit, I'm bouta nut already."

With no regard to my bulging belly, he lay down on top me and continued to pump in and out, all while grunting in my ear and kissing my neck.

Sex with Stoney lasted all of ten minutes, and I was happy as hell it was over. The moment he rolled off me and lay on his back, I hopped up and slipped my cellphone underneath my clothes so he couldn't see. I went straight into the bathroom to wash off, locking the door behind me. I had to figure out a way to get out of there.

Chapter 10

Barbee

It'd been days since we saw or heard from Sierra, and it was making us crazy. We didn't know if she was still breathing, or the baby for that matter. The news stations had become our new thing to watch just in case something did unfold. She wasn't even active on Facebook or Instagram, so that made it worse for us.

Corey and I had just finished eating breakfast at the kitchen table, but we were still sipping on the mimosas I made. Licking my lips, I sat the glass down in front of me.

"I don't know, babe, we may need to go ahead and file a missing person's report."

He shook his head no. "She's considered a runaway. They won't look for her."

"Well, we have to do something since we haven't found her yet, and I'm losing sleep behind this."

"I understand that, but I'm telling you what I know." Corey placed his elbows on the table with his fingers intertwined and rested them against his lips. I knew he was in deep thought whenever his brow raised.

"What are you thinking about?"

He moved his hands from his mouth. "Back in the day, when you used to run with Fox."

"What about it?"

"I need you to remember every motel y'all laid low in. Maybe we can find her there."

"How about any hotel, for that matter."

"Nah, they ain't gon' waste money on a good hotel. It's gon' be cheap."

"Yeah, I know, 'cause we stayed in every cheap motel in damn near every state." Pushing my chair out, I rose up from my seat, picked up the dirty dishes, and walked them over to the kitchen sink. "We need to get out and look for her now, 'cause I can't spend another day in here without knowing she safe and in her bed." I rinsed the dishes one-by-one and placed them into the dishwasher. "And this is the main reason I never told her about my past."

Corey got up from the table and brought the glasses over to the sink for me to rinse them out. "It's not your fault. She knows right from wrong, so stop that."

I turned around to face him. "I know, but just knowing she's following my footsteps makes that hard to do."

"We're gonna find her, so stop worrying," he assured me.

Lifting my chin, he kissed me gently on the lips. I reciprocated, becoming aroused immediately. My hands found their way to his waist, gripping him tightly. The beat of my heart increased, and my breathing became just a little bit heavier. His touch had that special effect on me.

But all of that came to an abrupt end when he broke our kiss and wiped my bottom lip.

"Why did you stop?" Whining wasn't necessarily my thing, but when I wanted something it happened so easily.

"'Cause we have to go, and if we start that now we will never leave this house." Corey stuck his hand between my legs and smiled. "Don't worry, I'ma dig up in there later on tonight." Then he walked away, whistling.

After I started the washer, I went into the room and grabbed my cellphone that was sitting on the dresser. A sudden wave of panic came over me when I unlocked my screen. I had two missed calls from Sierra and a text message.

I'm sorry. Please come get me. I'm at the Plantation Inn

with Stoney and I'm scared. Tell Corey
   Room 210

"Corey!" I screamed loudly as if he wasn't standing in the same room as me.

"What's wrong?"

"I just got a text from Sierra. Let's go."

Running to the closet, I grabbed my bag and placed my .40 in there. Corey grabbed both of his bangers and tucked them in the waistband of his jeans.

"Let's go." We rushed out the door.

***

Sierra

Hiding in the bathroom for thirty minutes was not what I had planned. The water was running so they would think I was taking a long shower. While I was pretending, I called and texted B, but she hadn't returned my calls or responded to my text. I guessed she was really mad at me. If only I had listened to her I wouldn't be in this predicament, but no, I had everything mapped out.

Boom, boom, boom!

"You better be in there taking a shower, 'cause you been in there for a long-ass time," Stoney shouted. I already knew it wasn't Trina banging on the door.

"I am."

"Well, hurry up."

The only thing I could do was take off my clothes and hop into the shower for real. There was no telling what he would do to me if he knew I was faking it. I stood underneath the waterfall and scrubbed my body with the cheap motel soap. The water from the showerhead mixed in with my own tears as I thought back to how this nightmare unfolded in the first place. All I was trying to do was get some money to pay off Dre's debt to Tokee's uncle so we could be together, but that plan has gone terribly wrong.

Turning off the water, I stepped from the shower and dried myself off with a towel. If Barbee didn't come get me soon, I didn't know what I would do.

Wrapping the hard towel around my body I walked out of the bathroom and into the room. The way I clutched the towel and took baby steps toward the bed displayed my insecurities. If it wasn't for me sneaking my phone into the bathroom, I would've remembered to bring in some clean clothes. Stoney was standing in front of Trina, but I couldn't really hear what was being said.

"Yo' bitch back, so you can go over there with her and get out my face." When she looked up at me, I knew that was being directed toward me, but I couldn't understand why she was so mad. Like I wanted to fuck him in the first place. I ignored her slick remark and slipped on a dress I had tucked away in my bag.

"G'on with that fuck shit, man." He touched her face, but she pushed his hand away.

"Don't fuckin' touch me."

"Who da' fuck you talkin' to like that?"

"I'm talkin' to you! Who the fuck you think I'm talking to?"

The next thing I saw was Stoney cock back and slap fire from her face. "Bitch, you better watch yo' muthafuckin' mouth. I don't know who you think you talkin' to, ho, but you better put that mouth in check before I wire that shit shut."

Trina's eyes stretched wide, but she didn't say a word, and I didn't either. That's exactly what she got for allowing him to do that shit to me. She had so much to say after the fact instead of

122

while the shit was happening to me. It's like she was stuck in a daze.

A few seconds passed, and she jumped up from her seat, decking him dead in the eye.

"Bitch, don't put your hands on me!" she screamed.

The next thing I knew, Stoney hit her with a two-piece combo. She stumbled, but she didn't fall. After catching her balance she rushed him, but he caught her with two more. Trina tried to fight him back, but he was too strong for her, and I didn't want no part of it. I sat back and watched Stoney beat her ass like she was a nigga on the streets who stole from him. And not once did she scream. I had to admit she was taking that ass-whooping like a pro.

When he finally got her on the ground, he gave a new meaning to putting your foot in someone ass. Stoney kicked her repeatedly in her ass while she balled up on the floor.

"Bitch, don't you ever try me like that again. I'll kill yo' fuckin' ass, ho. I feed you, and don't you forget it."

She could be heard whimpering, "I'm sorry. I'm sorry. Please stop. I won't do it again."

Stoney stopped kicking her and straddled her body, placing his hands around her throat with a death lock. "I know you won't, 'cause if you do, I will strangle yo' ass to death."

"I'm sorry," she gasped. The grip he had on her was so tight her eyes began to water. Using her nails, she clawed at his hands for him to let go, but that wasn't working.

"Bitch, how does it feel to look death in the eyes? Huh, ho? How does it feel?" He squeezed tighter.

Trina could no longer respond, and I could see the life in her slowly fade away. Her movement became slower and slower, and I had to do something. I slid off the bed slowly to make sure I didn't startle him. His gun was on the dresser, so I picked it up and aimed it at him.

"Let her go, now."

Stoney's head swiveled around. "And what the fuck you think you gon'–." He paused when he saw the gun in my hand.

"Turn her loose, now. I'm not gon' say it again." I rested my finger on the trigger. Never had I in my entire life shot a gun, but he was about to be target practice today.

He let go of her neck and rose to his feet. Trina hungrily gasped for air and rolled onto her side, coughing violently. There was this evil look in his eyes, and I knew at that moment I would have to kill him or be killed. "And what the fuck you gon' do with that?" He took a step toward me.

"Stay right there, Stoney. I'm serious." I took a step back, but he was steadily inching toward me. My hands were shaking from the heaviness of the weapon.

"You ain't gon' shoot me. You don't have it in you to pull that trigger."

The front door came crashing in, catching us all by surprise. Stoney spun around and came face-to-face with his match.

"But I will, nigga. It's in me, and you know it."

I was so relieved to see B and Corey come through in the nick of time. She had her gun aimed at him as she stepped in slowly. My brother closed the door behind them and walked in my direction with his heat in hand. Trina finally got off the floor and eased onto the bed.

"Oh, so she called you, huh?" Stoney grinned with his hands at his side. All that tough shit went out the window real quick.

"Sierra, you okay?" I nodded my head yes and lowered the piece. "Gimme the gun. You safe now." Loosening my grip, I slid my finger off the trigger and handed it to him. Corey sat it on the dresser and hugged me tight. All I could do was cry in his arms.

"I bet you never expected this either, huh, Stoney?" B was smiling at him, and that was a side of her I never knew. She looked crazy and deranged.

"He raped me, and she let it happen." I was crying, pointing in the direction of Trina and running toward Stoney at the same time. Corey tried to grab me, but not before I punched his ass in that slick-ass mouth of his. I landed blow after blow, and not once did he attempt to strike back.

"Calm down. Sierra, baby, we got this." Corey lifted me midair and carried me to the door.

"Don't move."

We heard a shuffling noise.

Pew!

By the time Corey turned around, Stoney's body was crashing to the floor. Never in my natural life had I seen an actual person killed in front of my eyes. I saw Chyna after she was dead, but to see it go down was a different story.

"Babe, what happened?"

Barbee shrugged her shoulders. "He tried to run for the gun, so I laid him out."

Trina was sitting in the corner of the bed with her knees pulled to her chest, crying. "Bitch, shut up!" I spat. "You wasn't crying when you let yo' nigga rape me." I tried to rush her too, but Corey was too quick this time.

"He's crazy. You saw what he did to me. What did you want me to do?" Spit was in the corners of her mouth, and snot ran from her nose as she cried.

"Protect me like I protected you. Fuck you thought?" That shit wasn't flying with me. This ho was supposed to be my friend, and she would let a nigga violate me like that?

"What should we do about her?" B looked in our direction. "I ain't going to prison behind killing this nigga." Corey had a grip on me, and he wasn't letting me go.

"Please," Trina begged. "I won't say anything. I swear. Just let me go."

Barbee turned to face her. "Now, why should I do that when you didn't help her? I'm confused."

"I couldn't do anything." Now she was rocking back and forth, crying as her teeth chattered. "I promise I won't say anything."

"Fuck her, Barbee. She ain't for me, and she gon' tell on us, that's a fact." Her being killed would be get-back enough for me. I just needed B to pull that trigger.

Barbee aimed her gun at Trina and fired a single round to the chest, and her body slumped over instantly.

"Slimy-ass ho." I walked over to her dead body and coughed up a huge glob of spit and hawked it on her.

"Wipe this shit off, and let's get out of here." Barbee slid her ratchet into her shoulder bag and helped me wipe down everything.

I went over to the closet and grabbed the bags. All the money, dope, and jewelry we stole was in there. I couldn't wait to get home and count it up. Today turned out to be a great day after all. I just had one more stop to make, then I would be home free.

Chapter 11

Corey

A few days had passed since we rescued my sister, and having her back home with us was such a huge relief. Just the thought of anything happening to her had me and Barbee on edge the entire time she was gone, and I would've never forgiven myself if she returned in a body bag. Right hand to the sky, I would've killed everybody involved.

Seeing B take action like that was a complete turn-on, although it was my job to protect my family. Before we went in she begged to take the kill because she owed Stoney for the old and the new, so I let her have that. But now it was time to take out one last person on my hit list in order for things to go back to normal.

Sliding through the hood, I pulled up at the gambling house and hit the horn twice. Everybody who was shooting dice looked up, but then one nigga walked toward my car and opened the door.

"What's up? You ready to do this shit?" He sat down in the passenger seat.

"Hell yeah."

Dre closed the door and I pulled off. We were on our way to tie up one last loose end. "Did you set it up?"

"I told him to meet us at the lake house." Dre looked in the backseat. "You got the shit."

"Yeah, it's in the trunk."

Dre rubbed his head and looked out the window as if he was in deep thought. Then, finally, he spoke. "How is Sierra and my baby doing?"

Taking my eyes off the road for a split second, I glanced over at him. The first thing that came to mind was to check the nigga, but then I remembered he was down for the cause. "They good, man. She still shook up a li'l bit, but she'll be a'ight. B been looking after her."

"Damn, I'll be happy when this shit over with. I miss my girl and my baby so bad. This shit has been pure torture these last few weeks."

I whipped the ride onto Sunrise Boulevard. "You really love my sister, huh?"

"Hell yeah." There was so much happiness in his voice. "You think I woulda went through all that shit with you, Tokee, and this nigga if I didn't?"

"I'm just checking, man, 'cause she means the world to me, and I'll lay any nigga down 'bout my baby."

At the end of the day, Dre had always been a solid nigga on my behalf, but when it came down to females he was on some other shit. "I'm fucked up 'bout her, and it's been like that since day one, but a nigga had so much shit going on I couldn't give her what she wanted." He rubbed his hands together. "But all that shit 'bouta change."

"All I'm gon' say is don't hurt my sister."

"You got my word, bruh. I'm gon' take care of her and my baby. She deserves it."

"Okay, we gon' see."

About ten minutes later we pulled up at the spot and parked the car, but no one else was there. I turned to face Dre.

"Aye, I thought you said this nigga was gon' be here."

My .45 was right on the side of the door. If this nigga was on that creep shit, I was gon' bust his head like a watermelon. With my eyes trained on him, I slid my hand to the side of the seat.

"He coming, just chill. This nigga gon' pull in after us. He always cautious when it comes down to shit like this. The nigga show up last to make sure he ain't being ambushed. Let's just get out the car and walk over to the lake so we in position." Dre opened the car door and got out, and I followed right behind him.

At the back of the car, I popped the trunk and pulled out the duffle bag. "A'ight, his ass better show. Grab that other bag."

"Damn, what's in this muthafucka?" He sat the bag on the ground.

"It's the tools, nigga."

"This bitch heavy as fuck."

"You gon' whine about it or carry the shit?"

"I got it, let's go."

We headed over to the bench close to the dock. No sooner had Dre slid the tools underneath the bench than I could see a set of headlights coming toward us.

"I told you he was coming." He stood erect as he adjusted the banger behind his back. "Showtime, my nigga."

I watched closely as Louie approached us with some big, black nigga I assumed was his bodyguard, judging by the way he walked close and observed his surroundings. He was carrying a bag. Once he was within a few feet of us, he paused.

"Let's make this quick, 'cause I have someplace to be." He looked at Dre. "Did you do a pat-down?"

"Nah, this my nigga. He cool. Ain't no funny shit goin' on."

That was my queue to set the record straight. "First off, I don't know you, you don't know me, and we don't trust, either. So ain't nobody givin' me a muthafuckin' pat down. I'm strapped, and I'm sure you are, too. I'm here to conduct business, and if you ain't 'bout that, then I can pack my shit up and haul ass."

Louie stood there in silence for a few seconds, scratching his ass like he wasn't the one calling all the shots. "Let's do it."

"Good, 'cause I thought we was playin' chess and not

checkers. Step into my office."

Louie walked in closer to the side where I was standing. Slowly I unzipped the duffle bag I was carrying, pulled out an AK-47, and handed it to him. He held it in his hands and examined the fine piece of steel. "Oh yeah," he laughed. "My soldiers can definitely use this. What else in the bag?"

I took a step back. "Take a look inside."

The bodyguard's attention was on his boss, and that's where he fucked up. I bent over to tie my shoe and came up busting.

Pow!

A single hollow-tip split him right between the eyes.

"What the fuck?" Louie shouted, and that's when I aimed my shit at his ass.

"Back up, nigga, and keep yo' muthafuckin' hands where I can see 'em." He inched back just a bit.

Dre took aim in my direction. "Nah, bruh, chill," he grinned.

This nigga had me confused as fuck. "What the fuck you doing? Aim that shit in this nigga direction." I pointed toward Louie.

Dre trained his eyes on his commander. "You know who that is?"

"Yeah, a nigga that lost his muthafuckin' mind, killin' my nigga like that thinking there won't be any repercussions for his actions."

"Nah, that ain't it. That's Sierra's brother."

He swiveled his head in my direction, and my aim was still on him, and Dre's was on me. Louie turned back to face his soldier. "Well, what the fuck you waiting on? Shoot this nigga."

Dre nodded his head. "A'ight." Then he pulled the trigger.

Boca! Boca!

The two rounds he fired took out Louie's kneecaps, sending him falling to the ground. "Argh, what the fuck you doing, Dre?" That nigga was in pain, crawling around on the ground

130

like the spineless snake he was.

Dre stepped in closer. "Remember what I told you that day at your house?"

The nigga nodded his head.

"Nah, tell me what I told you."

"That I signed my death certificate."

"You goddamn right, and ain't no nigga or bitch walkin' this Earth can make me abandon my responsibilities as a man. I warned you about threatening my girl."

Dre kicked the nigga in his side, but I kept my eyes on his ass, too. If I had to sink him, I would.

"It's all good, though, 'cause after we kill you, it's over between me and yo' niece. Then I will step in and take over your business and take care of my new family."

"Let's get rid of this nigga and bounce." By the time he finished going down memory lane, ain't no telling who was liable to pull up. I pulled the tool kit from underneath the bench and unzipped the bag, tossing Louie the chains. "Tie those around your ankle."

He hesitated like he didn't want to do it, so I gave him a little motivation and stepped on his knee.

"Argh," he grimaced. "Okay, okay."

Slowly, but surely he locked himself with the shackles. The next thing I grabbed was the cement block, and I connected it to the chain and secured the lock on that as well. I looked up at Dre. "Drag the nigga to the edge."

"Fa' sho."

Stepping behind his old boss, he grabbed him by the arms and pulled him to the edge of the dock. "Do this nigga, Corey."

For the threat he placed on my sister and the heartache he caused her, I put four bullets in his dome.

Boca! Boca! Boca! Boca!

His head exploded, and his body went crashing backward

into the lake. "Toss that nigga, too," I instructed Dre, referring to the bodyguard.

Once we were finished, we tossed the bag of tools in with him and grabbed the money bag that was left behind. On our way to the car, Dre stopped me.

"Aye, bruh, we good now?"

"Yeah, we good, bruh." We dapped it out and G-hugged. When we let go, he looked at me and laughed.

"What's so funny?" I needed to be in on the joke, too.

"I know you thought I was about to flip sides on you when I aimed that gun in your direction."

"Nah, I wasn't worried," I lied.

"It sho' looked that way, but that was get-back from the hotel, nigga. Now that we cool again, bruh, don't ever pull a gun out on me again."

"Treat my sister right and I won't have to."

"I got her from here, bruh. I promise."

***

Dre

The next day I was chillin' at the spot, contemplating my next moves. The news about Louie had just got out, and I knew that's why Tokee was calling me.

"What's up?"

"He's gone, Dre," she screamed. "He's gone."

"I know, but you gotta calm down. It's gon' be okay."

"No, it's not. He's not coming back." The pain in her voice ripped through my ear drums, but I didn't feel bad about it. Louie got everything he deserved. But if Tokee thought this was the end of her heartbreak, she had another thing coming. After her uncle was put in the ground, it would be a wrap for us, and I meant that shit.

"Where is Dre?"

"He's right here with me at my mama house."

"Is he around you right now?"

"Yes."

"Take him in the room to play or something, but don't have him around you in your condition. I'll be there soon."

"Where are you?" she sniffled.

"I'm at the spot. We trying to figure out who did this shit and the last person he was with. So gimme, like, an hour and I'll be there."

"Hurry, please, Dre. I need you."

"A'ight."

After hanging up the phone with her, I sat it down on the table and exhaled deeply. "That was yo' wife?" Leon was another one of Louie's workers.

"Yeah, man, she taking that shit hard. Now I gotta go home and deal with all this emotional shit."

"She did just lose her uncle, man, and she a female. They take death to the heart. Us niggas, we keep it moving 'cause this the life we live, and it's only two ways out. You know they don't understand that shit."

"I guess you right about that. I'll be there to console her after we wrap this shit up over here."

"I think you should just go and be with her for now. We can get down to the bottom of this shit another day. She need you right now, and besides, it ain't like we know who did it yet, anyway."

"Yeah, that's true." I nodded my head and thought about it.

"We need to look into them niggas that–"

Leon stopped talking midsentence, so I knew someone was behind me, but I wasn't sure who it was. My banger was sitting in my lap, but I didn't want to make a sudden movement and get my shit blown off. I stared Leon in the eye to get his attention, but he was focused on whomever was behind me.

Without visibly moving a single muscle, I was able to slide my hand down south and grip that steel. Once it was secure in my hand, I spun around and took aim on the person behind me, but I lowered it once I recognized her face.

She dropped a bag on the floor that made a heavy thud. *Boom!* Not knowing what to expect, I cleared the room out.

"Aye, gimme a minute, and lock the door behind you."

"A'ight." Leon got up from his seat and left the room. I waited for him to close the door before I said a word.

"What are you doing here?"

"Is that enough to clear your debt so you can leave your wife?" She kicked the bag closer to my feet.

I knelt down and unzipped the bag. Inside was money rolled up in rubber bands, but I was confused by her gesture.

"Sierra, what are you talking about?"

"I know why you left me, so I did what I needed to do to get you back."

"Who told you that?" 'Cause if Corey told her what was going on, I was gon' have to straighten him 'bout that.

"That night Corey went looking for you, I thought he killed you. I knew he wasn't gonna tell me, so I listened in on him and Barbee's conversation, and I heard him say you owe Tokee's uncle, and that's why you had to marry her."

All I could do was shake my head. I didn't know how to be mad at her for having that mind frame. "Sierra, what did you do to get this money?" Pinching the tip of my nose, I closed my eyes 'cause I could only imagine what she had to do to get it.

"It doesn't matter, just know I got it."

My eyes shot open, and I became instantly pissed with her. Using my right hand, I grabbed her by the chin. "What did you do? And don't tell me you fucked for it, 'cause if you did it's over between us, and I mean that shit."

Her eyes became glassy, and I felt in my heart that was what she did, so I released her and walked back to the table where I was sitting and just stood there with my back toward her. I could hear movement, but I didn't bother to turn around. Then I felt her hand touch my arm.

"Dre, that's not what I did. I swear it's not."

Just the thought put a few tears in my eyes, but I couldn't let her see me like this. "That's not an answer."

"Promise me you won't be mad."

"I ain't promising shit, so you might as well tell me 'cause I'm gon' find out."

"I was setting up niggas with this dude name Stoney that knows Barbee from back in the day when she first started."

My heart was so relieved that she wasn't fucking for money, 'cause I swear if she did I was gon' beat her ass. I wasn't worried about Corey 'cause I knew he would've agreed with me on that note. Before I turned around, I wiped my eyes.

"Damn, you did all that just for me?"

"I just wanted you to know what I would do to be with you." Not once did she make eye contact with me. She was too busy staring at the floor.

"You didn't need to do that. I'm a man, and I handled it on my own. What you did was dangerous. What if something would've happened to you and the baby? Then what?"

"I didn't think about that." Her voice was low, and she was acting like a child who was getting scolded by her father.

"Well, I appreciate the gesture, but I don't need the money. It's all good, so you keep it."

"And what about us?"

"We will be just fine."

"Does that mean you leaving her?"

"I have a few more loose ends to tie up, and then I'm all

yours, so start looking for a house."

Sierra jumped up and down in excitement. "I'm so happy, Dre. You just don't understand."

"Oh, believe me, I do."

This was the moment I had been waiting for, and it was finally about to happen. I lifted her up, placed her on the table, and kissed her like it'd been months since I saw her. Shit, it felt like an eternity, though. She was wearing a dress, and I couldn't wait to get up in there. My hands anxiously slipped up her thighs until I found her clit. Her soft lips were all over my neck while sucking and biting down on my skin. I didn't mind at all. I belonged to her, and vice versa. There wasn't shit Tokee could say about it now.

Sierra's pussy was so wet when I inserted two fingers and slid them in and out. Oh yes, she was ready for the dick, and I was ready to give it to her. My shit was rock hard in my pants, so I freed the nigga and put him in his favorite hiding place. It was tight, slippery, and warm, just like I left it.

"Ah," she moaned.

"Damn, I missed yo' ass." Rocking my hips, I slid in and out her wet opening. "Wrap them legs around my waist."

"Fuck me, daddy, please. I missed you, too."

I loved when she called me that shit. It turned a nigga on. Gripping her ass, I pulled her closer to me so I could dig all up in them guts. With a steady pace going, I bit down on her neck and stroked that pussy with all ten inches until I released every drop of nut that filled my heavy balls into that pretty, fat pussy of hers.

"Fuck," I shouted. "Damn, I love you, girl."

"I love you, too."

Chapter 12

Sierra

It had been four months since Dre and I became an exclusive couple, and I'm talking the whole shebang. Everyone in the city knew we were together, and everyone seemed happy for us except for one person, and there's no need to say her name. That bitch tried everything in her power to ruin what we had, but Dre wasn't going nowhere, and that's a fact. She even told him he needed a DNA test for our baby, but got mad when he said he wasn't getting one. She couldn't accept the fact she lost him to a high school student.

Dre pushed me through the lobby and out the double doors in the hospital wheelchair. I had given birth to our baby girl, Siyah Danaé Hamilton, two days ago. She was a spitting image of Dre with thick, curly hair and light brown eyes. Our little heavyweight came into the world weighing a whopping eight pounds and eleven ounces after a long night of painful, yet mind-blowing sex. I was ready to get her out of there, so we tried everything we could think of to make her exit the womb, and it worked like a charm because a few hours later I was having contractions.

He handed the valet attendant the ticket and we waited until he returned. An SUV pulled up first, and I was irritated because we were out there first.

"What's taking them so long? I'm hot and ready to go home." The medication I was on had me drowsy, and I was already irritable thanks to the damn stitches in my pussy. My fat-ass baby split my ass wide open, just like her daddy did me, but I wouldn't trade her for the world. When I first laid eyes on her, it was love at first sight.

"Relax, baby, our ride is here." He rubbed my shoulders.

Using my pajama top, I wiped my forehead and looked up at him with a screwed-up face. "Where, 'cause I don't see nobody?"

"That's you right there. You like it?" Dre had the biggest smile on his face, and I hadn't seen him smile like that since Siyah came out into the world screaming like we interrupted her vacation.

"What do you mean?"

"I bought this for you. Isn't this what you wanted?"

"Aw, Dre." My emotions were all over the place because I wasn't expecting a gift at all. My crybaby-ass was ready to pop out those tears at the drop of a dime. I placed my hand over my mouth. "I can't believe you got it for me." All I kept saying was how I wanted my first vehicle to be a BMW X6, cocaine white, and that's exactly what he surprised me with.

"You deserve it and so much more. What you were willing to do for me said a lot about you, and I know you not in it because of what I can do. You proved that to me so many times, and I love you for that." Then he hit me with the old forehead kiss. "And you gave me the daughter I always wanted."

Just above a whisper, I responded, "I love you, too."

Dre took the baby seat out of my lap and strapped her into the car before returning to me and carrying me to the passenger seat. Once I was secure in my seatbelt, he closed the door and came around to the driver's side. Scoping out the inside, I smiled because this was the best gift a girl at my age could ask for. Most girls my age got pregnant from boys our age, and they couldn't help them do shit. But not me. I had a grown-ass man in my corner who bought me a house and a truck. This was the life.

During the drive home, I caught myself constantly smiling at Dre. I couldn't have picked a better father for my daughter and a man for me. Things had become very rocky for us, and I

138

never thought I would see another day of happiness with him, but he proved me wrong. He made up for lost time every day we were together. Just having him present while I went through the most excruciating pain was a blessing. He cut Siyah's umbilical cord and held her first. A father is and will always be a girl's first love. Too bad I didn't know what that feels like.

Dre pulled up into the driveway of our four-bedroom, brown and beige stucco home and parked my new toy. I couldn't wait until I healed so I could get out the door and strut. Them hos at the group home would definitely see me soon.

In the meantime, I just wanted to get out of the car and into my king size bed and sleep. Siyah had a nursery we decorated in pink Coco Chanel, compliments of the best sister in the world, B. But she wouldn't be sleeping in there no time soon. Baby Dre had a room, also, which we decorated in Cleveland Cavaliers memorabilia. The fourth room was a guest room. We had a pool out back, so I was happy with the home I picked out.

My honey opened the door and took my hand, helping me onto my feet. Then he went into the back and grabbed the baby and her bag. Together we walked slowly onto the porch and into the house. I swear it felt like I walked a green mile to make it into the bedroom. When my head finally touched that pillow, I was ready to drift away. Dre put Siyah beside me.

"I have another surprise for you, so don't fall asleep just yet."

"What is it? I'm so tired, babe." My eyes were blinking constantly. He walked over to the dresser and came back with a folder.

"Take a look."

"Open it for me, please."

When he opened the folder, I just stared at the document. In his hand was a signed divorce letter, and my heart fluttered.

"I had this drawn up while you were in the hospital. All I

have to do now is wait for her to sign it, and once it's finalized the marriage will be over. She can keep the house 'cause I don't want it, and I'm not worried about child support 'cause he lives here half the time, so it's all good."

"That's the third best thing I've received this week." My cheek bones raised a little, and I was able to smile just a smidgen due to my drowsiness.

"I'm doing this for us and our family we starting, 'cause I need two more babies out of you."

"I don't think I can't handle pushing out any more little people."

"You got this baby. You went through childbirth like a champ." His laugh was so intoxicating, and I loved him so much. How could I say no to that?

"Okay, baby, whatever you want." Finally I closed my eyes and drifted off into sleep.

***

Barbee

The night air was cool enough to give a bitch wind colic like a newborn baby, so I pulled my black hoodie over my head to gain some warmth. It was two in the morning, and we were sitting in the rental car getting ready for some action. Blowing into my hands, I rubbed them together. I was convinced I was anemic or some shit.

"I'm ready." I looked over at Corey and smiled.

"You sure, or do you need to put on some makeup, too?" He was too tickled.

"Haha, you so funny."

"I'm just making sure the queen is equipped with all her necessities."

140

I pulled out my burner from under the seat and cocked it back. "This is the only accessory I need, sweetie."

Corey smiled and grabbed his ratchet, too. "I swear to God, I love to see you in action. You look so gangsta." He leaned toward me. "Give me a kiss before we go in."

Meeting him halfway, I gave him what he wanted and slipped in a little tongue action for my baby. That kiss warmed my body instantly like a cup of hot coffee. "We can finish this when we get home. Let's go."

Corey and I slipped from the car in our all-black attire and approached the house we had been staking out for the past few weeks. We knew this nigga's every move, and right then he was in that bitch sleeping like a newborn baby, sucking on his thumb.

There was a side door we approached and jimmied the lock on. That led us into his laundry room. We crept through that bitch quickly, but carefully to make sure we didn't knock over anything. The last thing we needed was to alert the bitch he had intruders. Loud snoring could be heard coming from the room, so we already knew that's where he was.

Taking the lead, Corey went inside first, but I was hot on his trail as he approached the bed and hit the lamp switch. The light was dim, but we could see everything. He hit the nigga in the stomach with the gun.

"Getcho faggot-ass up."

He winced in pain. "Argh, what the fuck y'all doing in an officer's house?"

"Nigga, shut up!" Corey spat and hit him over the head with the gun. "We don't give a fuck about that."

"Who the fuck are you? And what do you want?"

I stepped a little closer and took the hood off my head so he could get a good look at me. That nigga's eyes damn near popped out of their sockets. "Well, well, well," I smirked. "If it isn't Detective Punk-Ass Rhines. I told you I would get out. You never thought we would cross paths in the free world, huh?"

"How the fuck did you find my house?"

I rubbed my gun across his foot – the same exact one I used to murk Stoney's punk ass. "You'd be surprised at the connections I have." Tapping Corey on the shoulder, I slid in between him and the bitch and slapped him in the mouth with the butt of my strap. Teeth and blood flew from his mouth as he screamed out in pain.

"Bitch, you gon' die in prison." Blood was leaking from his mouth.

"Too bad you won't live to see it, bitch!"

Corey raised his gun and shot him in the shoulder. "Watch yo' muthafuckin' mouth, talkin' to my wife like that, nigga."

Just hearing him refer to me as his wife let me know we would get past the very situation that tore us apart. He fired four more shots into his body, and I watched closely as he took his last breath. I swear that was the best feeling in the world.

"We need to look for all the evidence he has on you and take his valuables to make it look like a robbery. The last thing we need is them assuming this was a way to get you off."

"Okay."

Both of us were wearing gloves, so we went through every drawer and room looking for anything of value or that would connect me to the case. By the time we finished ransacking the place, we had a briefcase full of evidence I knew nothing about, timepieces, and about ten grand in cash. The detectives on his case were going to need a clean-up crew after the way we left the place.

Chapter 13

Corey

After killing the detective who was trying to destroy Barbee, we lay low until I received the call confirming everything was clear. Although we took calculated steps to execute, we could never be too careful, and no matter what someone was always watching. Now, to say something would be another story.

My phone rang, and when I looked down at the screen, it was the chief calling. "Hello."

"Hey, son. We still on for today?"

"Yeah. I'm about to head up that way within the hour."

"Okay, I'll be waiting on y'all."

"A'ight."

When I hung up the phone, Barbee was still standing in the mirror. "Damn, B, we not having dinner with the President."

"I know that's right, 'cause if that was the case I wouldn't be going. Unless we were meeting Obama. First impressions are everything, and I need to look fabulous for the man saving my life."

"Trust me when I say he ain't nothing special."

Be sucked her teeth. "Any man who can keep me out of prison is very special."

As she applied her lipstick, I just stood there and shook my head. "Just hurry up so we can get up there on time and get this over with."

Spinning on her heels, she giggled and stepped toward me, adjusting my collar. "You need to have a better attitude about this saint, baby."

"Yeah, he a saint, alright. Call Sierra and see what's taking her so long. She was supposed to be here by now."

"Calm down. You do know she just had a baby not too long

ago, so she's not traveling light anymore."

"Well, shit, she got Dre, so she should be able to move a little bit faster than this."

"What about Sierra?" She walked in carrying the baby with baby Dre on her heels.

"Your brother here was just saying how slow you were moving and how long it was taking you to get here." B walked over and took the baby out her arms.

"Hey, Auntie Tooda Pie."

"Well, Corey, for your info, all four of us had to get ready."

"I see somebody lettin' you play step-mama." That shit was hilarious 'cause I could've sworn Tokee didn't want my sister around her baby.

"Bruh, I swear ever since I had the baby, she won't stop sending him over there, and you know we can't say no."

"The hell you can't," B snapped and rolled her eyes. "She just trying to make sure Dre don't forget about his son."

"Dre would never do that. He loves that boy. That's only in her sick and twisted mind."

"Where Dre at, anyway?"

"Outside getting the car seat and baby bag out my new whip."

My face twisted when she said that. "What new whip?"

"Dre bought me a new BMW."

Barbee was cheesing ear-to-ear. "What?"

"When I got out the hospital, he surprised me with it. I was going to call you and brag, but I wanted y'all to see it up close and personal, ya dig?"

"That's what's up. Congratulations on the whip."

"Thanks. Now all I need are some rims, and I think you should buy them since you didn't have to get me a car."

"I don' know 'bout all that."

"Girl, you know he ain't buying you no rims." Barbee was

rocking the baby and looking at me. "Ain't that's right? He only dress up his car."

The front door opened, and I was saved by the bell. "Let's go, 'cause Dre just walked in."

"You ain't slick, but we gon' finish this."

I walked out into the living room, and Dre was setting the baby stuff on the couch. "What it do, bruh?" I dapped him up real quick. Since he stepped up his game and did right by my sister, me and him was able to get back on track.

"Shit, I can't call it. Just trying to keep the women in my life happy."

"Shit, me too. And I only have one in my life, and she too much at times."

"I heard that, Corey." Barbee walked right up behind me. "Waddup, Dre?"

"Coolin', sis."

"Strap the baby in the seat so we can go."

B handed Siyah back to her mama. When she was done, we all headed outside and went to my car. Dre helped put the baby in.

"Call me when you get back."

When I looked over at them, they were in a deep lip-lock. "Aye, cut all that out. That's how she got here."

"Shit, it might be another one in there," Dre laughed.

"Hell nah." Sierra slapped his arm. "Corey, he lying. I can't have sex yet."

"We not having this conversation." I got in the car and closed the door.

Forty-five minutes later we were standing on the front porch of the chief's house. He opened the door with a huge smile on his face. "About time y'all showed up. I thought y'all was trying to bail out on me." He extended his hand, so I shook it with my free hand.

"Nah, we was waiting on slow-motion Sierra."

He looked over at her. "It's been a long time since I saw you. Do you remember me?"

"Yeah, I remember." Sierra wasn't too thrilled about the dinner, but she had questions for him, and that was her motivation to show up.

"And this is Barbee, the one you helping."

"Nice to meet you. Let me just say your mugshot didn't do you any justice."

"I would hope not." Barbee smiled and shook his hand as well.

"Well, come on in." The chief stepped back, giving us entrance into his home, and I had to admit it was laid out, but it definitely had a woman's touch to it.

"Right this way." We followed him to what I assumed was the family room.

Siyah was wide-awake when I sat her down. The chief bent down to get a good look at her. "So, this is my granddaughter? She is so beautiful. We have good genes." He raised his brow.

As soon as he said that, I looked at Barbee 'cause I never told her the chief was my father. She cut her eyes smoothly in my direction. Then she coughed. "Excuse me, your who?"

"My granddaughter."

"I'm confused." B folded her arms across her chest.

"I'm their father. You didn't know that?"

"No."

"Sorry, babe, it slipped my mind. This is me and Sierra's father, Chief Cornelius Belizaire."

"Oh, wow! I can see the resemblance." The sarcasm dripped from her voice.

"Just call me Neil. It's less complicated." The chief stood up. "I need to talk to the both of you in private, so step into my office. Sierra, make yourself at home. We'll be right back."

Barbee and I followed the chief into his study and popped a squat in the chairs across from his desk.

"Detective Rhines' murder case has been closed. The department believes he made too many enemies, that it's impossible to know who would want him dead. So, you're both in the clear." The chair squeaked as he rocked back and forth. "Barbee, the D.A.'s office has received a written statement from Rich stating he wants to take all charges, which excludes you in being convicted."

Her brow bent a little. I could tell she was trying to make sense of it all. "And does that mean I get off scot-free?"

"That could be the case, but it's really a hit or miss. There is a written letter in the file, but we would still see what the judge has to say about that." The chief played with the hair on his chin. "Did you retrieve all of the evidence in the home?"

"We took everything we could find, and that includes his cell phone," I spoke up for her.

"Did you bring that with you?" There seemed to be a little concern in his voice.

"Yeah, we got it," I answered with some hesitation in my voice.

"You need to destroy that ASAP."

"Gotcha."

"So, my next question is for you Barbee. Your co-defendant has a court date coming up. What would you like to do? Do you want to see what happens in court, or would you like to take care of it?" The way he expressed the word *you,* I already knew what he was getting at. And apparently she did, too, by the way she responded.

"I would prefer we handle it on our own. I don't trust him to carry out with his plan because he has a mental disorder, and he can flip it anytime."

The Chief nodded his head. "I'll hit my son with the details when we ready to move."

"Thanks. I really appreciate everything you doing for me, although I don't understand it."

He winked at her and bowed his head in my direction. "I'm doing it for him. I've done so much wrong in his life, so I'm just trying to make up for it."

"It's a start," she smiled back.

"Okay, well, I'm hungry. Let's get out there and eat."

Neil hooked us up with some lobster, steaks, crab legs, loaded potatoes and corn on the cob. A meal fit for a king. The fact he went out to display his sincerity was tugging at my heart, and I knew I needed to give him a fair shot at being a father to me and my sister, a grandfather to Siyah, and a potential father-in-law to B if things between us remained the same after we jumped these last few hurdles with her case. He deserved that much for all he had done for each of us at that table.

There was no denying how I felt about my girl, but there was so much still hanging in the balance, and we needed to iron out those kinks first. Maybe after the shit with Rich was dissolved, then I could move past it. It's different when a man cheats because he has no emotional connection and it's just sex. But when a woman cheats it's emotional, and no one could tell me anything different. Men and woman have and always will cheat for different reasons.

The slamming of the front door caught everyone's attention, so we all started to look around. As usual, my heat was on me at all times. I just never knew what or who I might run into.

Neil wiped his hands and mouth with his cloth and pushed his chair out to see who came through the front door, but before he could get out of his seat, Cruella de Vil was already standing there with the ugliest look on her face.

"Honey, who are these people?"

"What are you doing here?" From the sound of it, he wasn't expecting her at all. "I thought you weren't coming back until tomorrow."

"Well, we completed training one day early, so I decided to fly back home and surprise you. But you don't seem too happy about it."

"I'm just surprised, that's all."

Her eyes kept bouncing between me and Sierra as if she knew us. "So, who are your guests?"

"That's my daughter Sierra, my grandbaby Siyah, my son Corey, and his fiancée Barbee."

No one had to guess how she felt. Her actions showed it all. Out of nowhere she collapsed into our father's arms and held her head. Right then and there I knew that ho was drama queen.

"I think I need my medicine."

"I think you need a shrink," Sierra mumbled, but I heard every word she said.

"Y'all excuse me for a moment."

As soon as he helped her out of the kitchen, Sierra looked over at us, laughing. "That bitch is crazy. Ain't shit wrong with her."

"Tell me about it." I just shook my head and took a sip of my wine. That confirmed he didn't tell her he had been in contact with us.

A few minutes passed and he still hadn't returned, but I needed to drain the main vein, so I went looking for the bathroom. As I strolled down the hall, checking all the doors, I could hear loud yelling and cursing, so I went to the door to see what the commotion was about.

"You need to keep your voice down. I'm standing right here."

"No, you need to make them leave right now, and I mean

it."

"Those are my kids, and they are welcomed here in our home. I've let you keep them away from me for years, and I'm not doing it again." For the first time in my life it felt good to hear my father claim and defend us against this wicked bitch.

"Did you forget that you cheated on me and made those bastards?"

If I wasn't eavesdropping, I would step in and check that ho.

"Watch your mouth, 'cause you about to write a check your ass can't cash."

"Since when did you start caring about them? You never acknowledged those alleged children of yours. Why now?"

"It was because of you, but that has changed, and if you don't like it, then you can leave."

"Oh, so now you want a divorce? Is it because of what happened to their mother? Are you still upset because of what my brother did? Well, get over it. That bitch is dead and gone. You should've never been taking care of her and those kids behind my back. You didn't listen, so I made my brother kill her. I told him to kill the kids, too, but he didn't listen."

Things became silent, but I wasn't moving until I heard every bit of what she had to say.

"Don't look stupid like you didn't know, because you did. You're pretending not to know. After she died I wrote all about it in my diary, and you read it because I left it a certain way. So, if you cared so much about your children, then why didn't you say anything to me back then?"

Praying wasn't something I did, but I was hoping to God he wasn't about to admit he knew anything about it.

"You know what? You absolutely right. I did know, and I kept quiet because I was too blinded to see you for what you really were: a money-hungry, controlling, conniving, and ungrateful bitch."

150

"It doesn't matter what you think of me because you are just as guilty as me and my brother. You and I didn't pull the trigger, but our silence did enough damage to your precious-ass kids. They grew up without a father or mother."

"I'm done having this conversation with you, and I'm sick of this marriage."

My heart ached knowing this bitch set my mother up to be murdered, and what made matters worse was my father knew it all along and never said a word. If I didn't get out of there now, it was going to be a blood bath, and I was going to prison for the rest of my life.

"Sierra and B, let's go now. Get your shit."

"What's going on, Corey?"

The sincere concern in my baby sister's voice wasn't gon' make this any easier, but I didn't have the heart to tell her what I just heard. Not now or ever, for that matter. Just when I thought we were on a bridge to something new, that bitch got burned down just as quick. By the time he got away from that crazy bitch, we would be long gone.

Chapter 14

Rich

"Yo, what time is it?"

The transport officer looked at his stopwatch, then up at me. "Seven o'clock. Why, you wanna be on time?"

"That's the idea of it all."

My court hearing was at 8:30, and I was hoping for the chance to see Barbee in passing, if not in the same courtroom. Before today she probably hated my guts thinking I turned her in, but I was hoping she was smarter than that. Turning her in would mean I was confessing to a crime and going in right behind her. Those who know me can say I'm a liar, cheater, kidnapper, killer, and all of that, but a snitch wasn't a name I wanted on my resume out there in those streets. That just wasn't in my nature or bloodline.

The shackles I was in were uncomfortable as fuck. They made sure they put the bitches on extra tight because I was a high-risk escapee. Ain't no shame in my game. I'd buck whenever I got the chance. Especially now since I was getting a life sentence anyway. They knew I had nothing to lose, and that's why I had two guards and a driver for transport, and I was not allowed to be with other inmates. Somebody warned them about my record.

"How much longer is the drive? I'm all cramped up and shit."

"About a good thirty to forty minutes. You asking a lot of questions, like you got someplace to be."

"Yeah, court."

"Okay, well, sit back and enjoy the view. Pretend like you out sightseeing or some shit."

"Yeah, whatever."

This was about to be a long ride, so I eased into the corner of the van, put my head back on the seat, and closed my eyes. The best thing for me was to sleep until we made it there. There was no telling how long the hearing was about to be.

Boom!

A loud crashing sound snatched me awake from my power nap. When I opened my eyes, the transport van was spinning repeatedly in a full circle. I tried to hold on, but I wasn't strapped into a seatbelt, so I was being slung all across that muthafucka. Flying off the road at a high speed, we slid head-on into a tree. A thick cloud of smoke filled the van, causing me choke and cough. My body was wedged underneath the seat. Therefore, I couldn't move. The driver of the van was slumped over in the front seat. The two in the back were bleeding from their heads, and no movement could be seen. I tried to wiggle myself free, but that was a no-go.

Suddenly the door came ajar, and I could see a male figure climbing aboard. He called out to the driver and observed him. My guess was he was trying to see if he was dead.

Pow!

He fired a shot into his head. If he wasn't dead before, he was sure as hell dead now. The shooter slammed the door, so I knew he was headed to the back where I was. When the door flew open, the sunlight blinded my ass.

"Richard?" His gun was aimed at me.

"Yeah."

"You coming with me. Let's go." He caught a glimpse of the two officers and fired two shots into each of their domes.

My ass was still stuck, so he reached in and dragged me out by my shoulders and dropped me onto the ground.

"Go wait by that tree."

It wasn't a full two minutes before the explosion went off, blowing the van up into smithereens. We walked up a half-mile before I was thrown into the back of a black Tahoe.

"Aye, where you taking me?" This nigga ain't told me shit since he pulled me from the smoking van.

"Just shut up and ride."

This truck ride seemed long as fuck, and I was tired of lying down in the back. I was ready to get out the damn cuffs. It felt like I had been in that bitch for an hour. Then suddenly the driver hit the brakes, causing me to hit my head on the door.

"This some bullshit," I mumbled.

When the truck came to a complete stop and didn't move, I knew it was time to get out, so I rolled over to keep from falling when he opened the door. When he snatched the door open and pulled me out, I was confused as fuck. My first thought was, *what the fuck am I doing at a barn?*

It smelled like shit and hot garbage out there. The silencer pushed me like we were in the wrestling ring. He was lucky I didn't fall or we would have had some major fuckin' problems. I was just curious to see what the fuck was goin' on. I had been looking for my wife for the longest, so I wasn't sure if the lawyer Manny hired put this together or what. All I knew was the anxiety was killing me.

The shed seemed to be a little up to date, so whoever owned this muthafucka took their farming seriously. I saw a few pigs, chickens, and a horse stable. The door swung open like they knew we were standing there waiting to get in.

"Go inside." He pushed me again.

"Aye, you gon' stop pushing me, too? I don' know what the fuck yo' problem is, but you need to tell me what the fuck I'm doing in a damn barnyard and not in court."

"I can help you with that answer." Stepping from the shadows was a well-dressed older man I had never seen a day in my life.

"Well, shit, let's get to it. Y'all done made me miss court already, so what's up?"

"I have someone who wants to see you and thank you personally for all you've done."

"What?" Now this nigga was playing games, and I wasn't on that shit.

When Barbee walked into the room with that nigga, my heart dropped. I just knew when I saw her again that nigga wouldn't be nowhere in the picture. That muthafucka fooled my ass. Instantly I started to grit my teeth out of frustration.

"Now it all makes sense, why I'm here. You want to thank me for taking the charges for you, huh?"

Barbee walked up to me, but she kept herself a good distance to make sure she wasn't too close to me. "Yes and no. First of all, I need to know how in the fuck they got the video you deleted out your phone."

"I deleted it, but I still had a copy in a backup file just in case you tried to flip it on me. When I got into a car accident, they confiscated my phone and found it."

"And how do I know you didn't turn it in to get back at me?"

"Come on, Barbee, you know me better than that. You know I ain't no snitch. If I wanted you to go down, I wouldn't be taking your charges right now."

Her punk-ass nigga stepped up and passed her a gun. "Fuck all that, let's get this shit over with."

After all we been through, she still couldn't see that I did love her. My guess was she was too blinded by this smooth-talkin'-ass nigga on the side of her. "Don't listen to that nigga. We got history, and you know how I feel about you. All that shit I did to you, I didn't mean it, and you know my condition."

"Shoot this nigga!" The nigga was mugging me hard, but no matter how he felt, she still had that bitch at her side, so I knew

156

she was thinking 'bout that shit.

"You know me better than anyone in this room. Think back to when we met, our trip to Jacksonville. Do remember what you told me? You said you loved me, and you no longer wanted to be with this nigga."

"Rich, I never said that, so stop lying." Barbee raised her gun and aimed it at my chest. Maybe she would smoke me after all. But I'd be damned if I went out like a sucker.

"Tell this nigga how we fucked all weekend the night you tried to get away. The number of times I ran up in that pussy raw. How you sucked my dick on the highway? Better yet, tell that nigga that when you got shot, you was pregnant with my baby."

The next thing I knew, Corey raised his gun and let off so many shots.

***

Corey

It felt like I let off a hundred rounds into that nigga's chest cavity. The shit coming out his mouth had me furious, and the fact she couldn't pull that fuckin' trigger. I done seen her on one too many occasions split a nigga wig with no hesitation, and when she got around to this nigga she froze up. This was gon' make me re-evaluate everything we done. I couldn't stand to look at her right then, so I walked away.

Neil was standing there, giving orders as usual. "Pick that body up and bring it out here."

The barn had a back door, so I went and stood there until they were close to me. We walked outside to a muddy area and he whistled. B wasn't too far behind.

Not even thirty seconds later we saw two big-ass boars

come out. "What the fuck?"

"If you wanna get rid of a body without leaving no evidence, you get a boar hog to do the job for you. These babies will eat the hell outta his ass and digest the bones."

The way he patted me on the shoulder made me uncomfortable, and I knew it was because of what I heard them say the night we were at their house.

"Drop the body in the pen."

One of his henchmen tossed Rich's body over the wooden fence like he was a sack of potatoes. As soon as his body hit the mud, the hogs went crazy for feeding time. "I ain't fed them in two days, so they starving.

The sight of them tearing into his flesh had me nauseous, so I went back inside the barn to get my thoughts together. There was a crate by the front door, so I sat on it and put my head down in my lap. The creaking sound of the door didn't bother me one bit 'cause I had a feeling I knew who it was. My eyes were open, so I could see her feet in front of me.

"Corey, I hope you don't believe any of that shit he said, 'cause it's not true."

She grabbed my arm, but I snatched it away from her and stood up. "At this point, B, I don't really care. I did my part, and that was to make sure you didn't do a life sentence."

Tears filled her eyes, and normally that would move me, but not today.

"Corey, please."

She was begging and trying to hold my hand, but I kept resisting her.

"Don't do this. You know I love you."

"I don't know shit." My mind was fucked up, so I turned to walk away. I knew I needed to get out of there and go sit in the truck until they were ready. As soon as I opened the barn door, she pushed it closed to stop me from leaving.

"Corey, you always run away and you never wanna talk. We need to talk about what happened."

It was hard to look her in the eyes, but I needed honest answers. "You loved that nigga?"

"No."

"Don't lie to me."

"It's the truth."

"Did you fuck the nigga?"

"Corey, stop please."

I hadn't seen her break down and cry that hard since her sister was killed. Spit bubbles formed at the sides of her mouth, and the tears were falling heavily.

"It's a simple question: did you fuck him?"

"Yes, but that's only because –"

All I needed to hear was yes, and I put my hand in her face quickly to stop her from talking. There was nothing she could say or do to justify what she did.

"Save it, 'cause I don' wanna hear it."

When I turned my back on her, she grabbed me with force. "It didn't mean anything, I swear. I didn't have a choice. He forced me to sleep with him, and I never sucked his dick."

And that was the moment when shit got bad. My hand wrapped around her neck and I pushed her against the wall. She was still wailing non-stop, but I kept on squeezing.

"I just watched you freeze up 'cause you couldn't kill your real baby daddy, and you want me to forget about that?" I spoke through gritted teeth. I was so close to her face I could feel the air coming through her nose. As soon as I said that, I regretted it because that was a terrible loss for us, but it didn't dismiss the fact I was hurting just as bad as she was.

"Corey, please let me go. And you know that was your baby." Her voice was low, barely above a whisper, and I knew I had gone too far. Since we'd been together, I never placed a hand on her, but all that changed quickly.

"This is how I know shit is bad between us, because I just put my hands on you. But I'ma let you go, and I'm gon' walk away from this. I'm begging you to stay inside, 'cause I need time to cool off and think."

When I removed my hand from her throat, she took a few deep breaths to regulate the pace. Her chest was moving up and down rapidly. Once I realized she was okay, I went outside to catch mine.

Chapter 15

Tokee

It was not a good day for me, and I felt like I was dying a slow, painful death. I got the worst news of my life. It all started with me waking up to an empty bed because Dre left me a few months ago. After my uncle's funeral, he moved out of the house without saying a word to me. So I pulled myself from the bed and got Li'l Dre dressed for school, and then myself. On my way out, I opened the door and standing there was a uniformed cop.

"Are you Tokee Williams?"

I was a little discombobulated because that was my maiden name. "Yes, that's me." I placed my hands on my hips. "Why?"

"You've been served." He handed me an envelope and walked away.

With Dre at my side, we stepped onto the porch and I closed the door and locked it. My curiosity was killing me, so I got us to the car quickly and buckled us in. I opened up the envelope and pulled out the paperwork. My hands started to tremble and my eyes filled up with tears. I slung the contents to the floor of the passenger seat and punched the steering wheel.

"I can't believe this muthafucka filed for a divorce after all we've been through," I cried.

"What's wrong, Mommy?"

My baby was so innocent, and I felt so bad I was losing it in front of him. Quickly wiping the tears from my eyes with my hands, I rubbed them on the jeans I was wearing and got myself together. "Mommy's okay, baby. I'm sorry I scared you."

"Where's Daddy?"

I could see my son looking at me through my peripheral vision. He knew something was wrong, and it amazed me he knew it was about his daddy. "He's away at work, but I'll call him for you later, okay?"

"Okay." Dre picked up his toy off the seat, then looked back up at me. "Don't cry, Mommy. Daddy will be back."

Holding back the tears, I smiled. "I don't think so, baby."

After I dropped Dre off to daycare I bawled my eyes out as soon as I made it back to the car. My husband and I had been together since middle school, and I couldn't believe he would throw it all away behind some teenage pussy. I needed to talk to him, but I couldn't let him hear me crying because he wouldn't show up, so I sent him a text.

Tokee: Can you come by the shop please? It's important
Dre: For what?
Tokee: It's about Dre and the new arrangements
Dre: We can discuss that over the phone
Tokee: Please Dre in person now
Dre: Yeah

Although he had been gone for a while, I never changed his name from "Husband" in my phone. I was always holding onto hope we would reconcile. But boy, was I wrong.

An hour later, Dre was standing in front of the glass door. He had a key to the shop, but he left that behind when he walked out of my life. I took a deep breath and let him in. The scent of his cologne tickled my nose, and I damn near wet myself. Gucci Guilty was my all-time favorite. That would guarantee any nigga the panties. It was obvious he was happy. His chocolate complexion was shining, and he had picked up a little weight. He wasn't fat; that shit was just right.

"What's going on, Tokee?"

162

The way he said my name was a dead giveaway I no longer had his heart. His tone was very dry. Back when we were happy, it sounded so different.

"Nothing much, you know. Maintaining and trying to keep myself together." I walked over to my station, but he kept himself at a distance.

"So, what about the new arrangements?" Dre got straight to the point, letting me know he wasn't there for small talk.

"So, you got the daughter you always wanted. How is she? Does she look like you?"

Dre shook his head, and the mean mug on his face was serious. "I know that's not why you called me here, so what's up?"

"I can't ask about my husband's illegitimate child?"

"Listen, if you don't get to the point of this visit, then I'm leaving." It was evident he didn't want to be bothered or questioned. "I don't have time for the bullshit."

I found the strength to pick up the envelope from the counter and address him. Waving it in the air, I yelled, "Dre you filed for divorce. How could you do this to me?"

"Man, I ain't been in that house in months. Why you so surprised? You had to know what was coming next."

The pain I felt at that moment had to be the worst of all. I wanted to lay down and die right then and there.

"Are we going to discuss Dre's arrangements or not?"

"Yes, but we need to sit and talk about this. Can we talk about this in my office, please?"

"Why can't we just talk about it right now?"

"Because my stylists will be in here soon, and I don't want them in my business." I could sense he was trying to be patient with me.

I led the way to the office, and he sat down with his hands folded. "So, what's up?" he asked, as calm as could be.

I could feel myself become emotional, but it was now or never. "I've been doing a lot of thinking, and Dre, I'm going through hell without you, and I'm tired of not being with you. This whole thing is driving me crazy." The tears were falling constantly as I sobbed and talked. "I love you so much, and I don't want to be with anyone else. I can't pull myself to move on. I've turned down every man who has approached me, and it's because of you. I thought you would come back to me."

Dre had this blank stare on his face. He held his head back, rubbed his hands over his face, and exhaled deeply. I detected that he was mad, but when he spoke he was still calm.

"Come on, Tokee, please don't do this to me right now."

"Don't do this to you?" I yelled. "What the fuck is that supposed to mean? Do you have any idea what I'm going through?"

To my surprise, he remained calm, and I assumed it was because he was aware of my pain.

"Believe me when I say I understand how you feel, but you need to feel where I'm coming from. I have a baby I have to take care of, and I can't do that if we're together."

"What am I supposed to do without you?" I cried hysterically.

"I can't tell you what to do, but I can tell you this: I have no ill feelings toward you, and I'll continue to be there for you and Dre."

"You won't even fuck me anymore."

"Fuckin' you ain't gon' make the situation no better. That will only complicate things, and you know we can't be together like that."

"Why?" I was distraught and emotional, and I couldn't handle his rejection. The pain he subjected me to had me weak. "Answer me."

Dre stood up to leave, but I blocked his path. "Why can't

you be with me?" The one thing I hated was repeating myself, and he was just blatantly ignoring me.

Not once did this man look me in my eyes. "I just can't. I'm sorry," he mumbled.

"What the fuck do you mean by that?" Before I knew it, I was throwing wild punches at his face. Dre managed to block some of them, but I did catch him in his lip, drawing blood. "Why? Tell me why?" I screamed.

Dre licked his lip, and I could see the darkness in his eyes. He grabbed me by my arms and shook me. "Stop it!" he yelled. "I ain't goin' through this shit with you."

"Tell me why?" I was trying to break free from his tight grip.

"I'm with Sierra now, and we live together. That's who I wanna be with."

"You just givin' up on us like that?" My breathing was heavy, and I could feel the saltiness from the snot that touched my lips, but I didn't care. All I wanted was my husband back. "Dre, please don't leave me."

"I'm sorry Tokee, but it's over." He finally let go of my arm.

Using my left arm, I wiped my face. "Do you know what your son asked me today?" I sniffled. "He asked where was his daddy, and why he hasn't come home yet." I stepped closer to him and put my face close to his so he could see my pain and feel how I felt. "He told me to stop crying because Daddy will be back." Dre looked away from me and shook his head from side to side. "Do you know how that made me feel?"

"My son will be okay 'cause I will talk to him, because you played a major part in this."

"How? I'm not the one who cheated. It was you cheating with that young ho."

Dre bit his lip, and I knew I pushed a button 'cause the last time I called her out her name, he was pissed with me. His fist was clutched so tight I just knew he was about to hit me, so I backed up.

"I'ma let you have that because I love that young ho to death. She do shit you wouldn't do. I don't have to beg her to suck my dick 'cause she get to it with no problem. I would've left you off her head game alone. My baby is a bonus."

"Fuck you, Dre." I turned on my heels to walk away from his cruel and evil ass.

"Nah, there's more. I want you to hear all of this. I never wanted to get married, and the only reason that happened was because I got robbed for your uncle shipment, and he said if I married you he would forgive my debt."

That last sentence knocked the wind out of my ass. I doubled over in pain because I couldn't believe my marriage was built on a lie. "I don't believe you."

"If you don't believe nothing else, pay attention." Dre tapped his temple with his finger. "Why you think I left after he got killed? My debt died when he did, and so did my love for you. The day he was buried was the day I buried my feelings for you. Now take that to the bank. I'm out."

Dre walked past me without taking a second look at me. "Dre, wait, please."

I could hear that movement stop, so I looked up and he was standing by the door.

"What?"

"I can't believe I went through all of that shit for nothing." After everything he said to me, there was nothing but pure hate in my heart and eyes. I knew he could feel me shooting daggers straight through him. If looks could kill, he would've been stretched out on the floor. "I should've let you die. He told me about the shipment, but I told him not to kill you because I love you."

"Well, you should've let him do it. As of right now, I'm dead to you, so keep that in mind."

Dre walked out the door and left me feeling broken, confused, and worthless. I sat down at my desk and pulled out my prescription bottle, dumping them eagerly into my hand. I discarded the entire bottle and lay down on my desk, praying God would take me out of my misery.

Destiny Skai

Chapter 16

Dre

The constant ringing from my cellphone woke me. I was trying to take a nap with my lady and baby. Slipping my arm from under Sierra's head, I picked the phone up from the nightstand. Squinting my eyes, I saw it wasn't a number I recognized, but I picked it up anyway.

"Yeah."

"Dre, this Tokee sister."

Now, I wasn't sure why she was calling, but something was telling me it was about some bullshit. But for her sake, I hoped not.

"Hold on." I walked out of the room so I didn't wake up my sleeping beauties. "What's up?"

"Tokee is in the hospital."

That had me confused because I just saw her a few hours ago. "For what?"

"Apparently she overdosed on prescription pills."

"When?" I walked into the living room and sat down on the couch.

"What did you do to her?" she snapped. This bitch just assumed I did something to her crazy-ass sister.

"Hold up, I didn't do shit to her," I snapped back. "I don't know what you talkin' 'bout, and if you called to blame me, you barking up the wrong muthafuckin' tree."

She blew her breath into the phone like I was aggravating her. "Now, if you're finished, I have something to say."

"What, man?" I leaned back and prepared for the slick shit about to slip from her loose lips.

"From day one, you have been giving her nothing but broken promises. I don't understand why she fell for the bullshit

Destiny Skai

in the first place. She really thought you were going to be with her after all the shit you took her through. Now you have a newborn baby, and it's fuck her. I think it's fucked up, if you ask me. While you over there pretending to be in love and acting like this is your first child, I suggest you go and get you a paternity test."

"Hold up." I tried to speak, but the bitch wouldn't stop talking.

"I told her dumb ass not to get married, but no, she didn't listen to me. Now you done went and started a new family, and she around here looking stupid. That's really fucked up, how you did her, Dre."

It was clear to me Tokee had been talking to her sister about our marriage. Out of all the people to vent to, she confided in her jealous, messy-ass sister. She had it twisted. This ho must've had fish grease for breakfast, talking that slick shit. That wasn't gon' fly with me.

"Check this out, homegirl, you not about to talk to me all greasy and shit. You jaw-jackin' 'cause you think I won't reach out and touch you, but you better walk light, 'cause you treading in dangerous water. You trying to go off about somethin' that don't concern you or what you know nothing about. This between me and Tokee, not you. It's more to the story than what she's telling you."

"Yeah, and I understand that, too. But she did make a big-ass sacrifice for you, in case you forgot about that."

"Here you go again, not mindin' yo' fuckin' business."

"You damn right, here I go again, because I am sick of this shit. Dre, I'm going to say this, and I'm done with it."

"Well, be muthafuckin' done."

"The hold you have on her is disgusting. You brought her all the way down, and it's amusing to you. What type of man does that?"

170

"The same type of man you wanted to fuck, but I shut you down. That's the real reason you mad, 'cause I wouldn't fuck you, let alone suck my dick. Now keep rappin' and watch me blow up your spot."

"Whatever, man."

"What hospital she in?" I wanted this bitch off my line.

"I'm serious, Dre, leave her alone if you're serious about building your family. You need to stop all contact with her, because if not, someone is going to end up hurt."

Since she didn't answer my question, I didn't bother to respond. I bammed it on her ass, sat my phone down on the coffee table, and buried my head in my hands. When I looked at the floor, I could see Sierra's feet.

"Is everything okay?"

I nodded my head, but I didn't look up.

"What happened?"

Dropping my hands, I made eye contact with her. "This muthafucka overdosed on pills, and now she in the hospital."

"Who?"

"Tokee."

"Why did she do that?"

And there it went. I had to explain to her what happened. "She texted me this morning saying she wanted to talk to me about the new arrangements with Dre. But when I got there, she was crying about the divorce papers being served."

Sierra placed her hands on her hips. I knew she was mad because one of her brows was up and the other was down. Whenever I pissed her off in the beginning of our relationship, her bottom lip would also curl. "So, when were you going to tell me about your little pop-up visit with motor-mouth Maebelle?"

Ever since I told her Tokee told her uncle our business, she gave her a new name, saying she talked too damn much, and that was a fact.

"I was gon' tell you, but I didn't want you to get mad for no reason. All she wanted was answers about the divorce. I told her what it was and she couldn't handle it, so I guess she trying to kill herself."

"Yeah, whateva."

"You know what it is, so calm down."

"So, who called you?"

"Her sister, and that's why I left the room, 'cause I didn't wanna wake you and the baby up."

Sierra rolled her eyes. "Yeah, okay."

"Come on, baby, don't do that. You know I can't stand her ass. I had to cuss her out."

"For what?"

"'Cause she always in my fuckin' business. She worried about what I got going on over here with you."

"Them hos always talkin' about me." She clapped her hands in between every syllable. "But let them know I ain't pregnant no more, and I want a bitch to run up. It will be an instant replay of when I beat her ass at y'all fake-ass wedding."

My baby was crazy, but I loved the hell out of her ass. "Chill out, bae, ain't nobody runnin' up on you. I'll slap any one of them bitches 'bout you."

"That's what I know."

I got up from the couch with my phone in my hand, and Sierra rolled her neck.

"Where you going? You trying to go to the hospital? 'Cause if you are –"

I had to stop her right there. "Chill, I'm going to pick up Dre from daycare."

"Well, I'm going."

"If I go up there, I may have to slap her sister down. It's all good, though, 'cause I'ma send B up there." I dialed her number.

172

She picked up. "What's up, Dre?"

"Aye, I need you to do me a solid."

"What's that?"

"Tokee swallowed a bottle of pills and she in the hospital. Can you slide up there and check on her for me, please? 'Cause if I go up there right now, I'm goin' to jail."

"Yeah, I can do that. What hospital she in?"

"I think Memorial, but her stank-ass sister wouldn't tell me, so you gon' have to call up there."

"I gotcha. Where is my sissy and niece?"

"She right here, all in my mouth, and the baby asleep."

"Tell her I said hey and kiss my baby for me." B blew kisses into the phone.

"She said hey, baby."

"Hey, sissy-poo. I miss you." Sierra was talking loud like the baby wasn't trying to sleep.

Barbee laughed. "Tell her I miss her, too, and I'll stop by."

"Okay, just let us know when you coming."

"I'll call you when I leave the hospital."

After I ended the call, we got dressed and headed out to pick up my son.

***

Barbee

The sixth floor of the hospital was completely silent, but the sound of my heels clicking disturbed the peace. As I walked into the room, Tokee's eyes were open and she was looking toward Melissa, one of her stylists.

"What is that noise?" she mumbled. I could hear the annoyance in her voice.

"Oh, that would be me." I smiled and walked closer to her

bed.

Tokee looked frail, her smile was faint, and her eyes were very dark. "I'm surprised to see you here." Her voice was groggy.

"I had to come and check on you." I sat my purse down on the table next to her.

"Who told you I was here? Was it Dre?"

I nodded my head. "Yes."

A single tear slipped from the corner of her eye onto the pillow. My heart went out to her 'cause I could only imagine the pain she was going through. I placed my hand on her head and stroked it gently. "Tokee, baby, everything is going to be okay."

"No, it won't. You just saying that."

"You have to learn when to let go. Dre has moved on, and you should do the same." I hated to say this to her, but she needed to hear it. "He's not coming back to you. He's with Sierra now, and that's who he chose, so you need to get over it. And trying to kill yourself is not going to help. Think about your son, because he needs you."

Tokee moved her head back. I guess she didn't want me to touch her anymore. "That would be very convenient for you, huh? If I just walked away without a fight. But if you think I'm giving Dre up to some young, hot, Cheetos-eating bitch, you got another thing coming, and so does Dre. Is this why he sent you here?"

Deep down inside, I wanted to snatch this sick-in-the-head ho out of the bed and beat her ass. But I'd charge it to the game this time, since she was ill and on medication. "I'm going to pretend you didn't just try me like that, but since you want to get right to it, let's do it. What the fuck is wrong with you? You letting a nigga have that much control over you that you don't know how to walk away. I didn't introduce them to each other, and you know that shit, so you can stop blaming me for the

174

issues that went on with y'all before the wedding. You thought 'cause he changed yo' last name he was gon' change with it?"

"Just stop." She looked over my shoulder, and when I turned around Melissa had this surprised look on her face. "She doesn't know."

"Tuh." At this point it didn't matter. Hell, maybe someone else needed to tell her how ridiculous this shit was.

Melissa stood up. "I'm going to walk down to the cafeteria so the two of you can talk in private. Do you want anything?"

"No, I'm good."

As soon as Melissa was out of earshot, I turned back to Tokee, who was now lying on her back. Her body language clearly said she didn't want to be fucked with, but that wasn't going to stop me from saying what I needed to say. "Now that she's gone, we can cut to the chase and get straight to the point. What is your problem?"

"I don't have a problem."

"Sweetheart, have you taken a look around you? I would definitely say you do."

"I don't want to talk about it."

"That's the problem, you need to talk about it. And I bet if you did, you would feel much better. Take responsibility for your failed marriage." The tears were flowing freely down her face, so I stepped closer to her and wiped them from her eyes. I guess the medication they provided wasn't strong enough to ease this pain. "Tokee, what are you doing to yourself?"

"I don't know. I just want the pain to go away," she whispered.

I felt a little bad for her because I knew how much she loved her son. However, I had zero understanding on how she could allow a man to tear her down so bad. She wouldn't date, flirt, fuck, or be friends with anybody of the opposite sex, and Dre had been gone for months now.

"What pain?" I already knew the answer to that question, but I wanted to hear her say it.

"All of it."

"I can't help you if you don't talk to me."

She stared into my eyes and didn't blink once. "You can't help me. No one can help me, can't you see that?"

"Is that what you want to believe?"

"It's what I know."

This was not my close friend I genuinely loved like a sister, and it broke my heart to hear her basically say her life was over and there was no coming back.

My thoughts were interrupted when Tokee began to speak to me in a soft tone. "You can let yourself out. My meds are kicking in." She rolled over so she wouldn't have to face me. Granting her wish, I stepped back and grabbed my purse so I could leave.

"Before I go, let me tell you something. You can lay in this bed feeling sorry for yourself, because I don't. My only concern is baby Dre. It's bad enough he lost the luxury of having a two-parent household, but the worst part is he about to lose his mother because she thinks death is easier. I remember when you were crying on my shoulder about what he was putting you through. I told you y'all needed time apart, but then a few days later you come back and say y'all getting married. I knew it wasn't gonna last, but you insisted on being married. Dre has complete control over you, and he's not even your husband anymore."

Hurting her feelings was not what I came there for, but it was time she heard the truth. She had a child she was responsible for, and there she was trying to take her own life. I walked out of the room and didn't look back. Hopefully she would take my advice into consideration.

Chapter 17

Sierra

For some reason I never saw myself as a step-mother, but since this crazy-ass bitch decided to take a break from motherhood, I didn't have a choice. I loved Dre, and if I had to take care of his son, then so be it. That night I cooked dinner for us. I kept it simple by making Li'l Dre's favorite meal: spaghetti. I had to do whatever it took to keep his focus off his mother and make him comfortable.

After dinner I got up to clean the table. "Dre, are you finished?"

With a mouth full of food, he looked up at me and nodded his head. "Uh-huh."

I picked up his plate. "Okay, well, we're gonna get you ready for a bath, and then it's bedtime, okay?"

He swallowed his food. "Okay."

"Baby, I'll give him a bath and do the dishes. You've done enough." Dre was sitting at the table holding Siyah. He was everything I could've ever asked for in a man.

"You sure? 'Cause I can go ahead and get him ready."

Dre smiled at me. "Nah, I don't want you tired. I need you to be ready for me when the kids go to sleep.

All I could do was laugh. "I knew there was a catch to that."

"You already knew." Dre stood up and walked toward me. "Here, get the baby so I can get him ready."

Grabbing the towel from the counter, I dried my hands off and took my princess from his arms. "Come on, sugar, so your daddy can get your brother ready."

It was after 10 o'clock by the time we were settled. Li'l Dre didn't want to sleep alone, so his daddy had to lay down with him until he finally fell asleep. Siyah seemed like she was cock-blocking, 'cause all she did was smile, coo, and look around.

"These kids really wore me out. I'm tired, babe." I stretched out across the bed after getting out of the shower. My body was wrapped in a towel.

Dre was sitting on the side of the bed, but he got up once I lay down. "I know, and that's why I said I will take care of everything else."

He grabbed the lotion bottle and came to where I was and pulled the towel off, exposing my naked body.

"It's cold in here." My body shivered.

"Don't worry, I'm about to change all that." Dre removed his clothes, but he left on his boxer briefs. My baby was shaped like a model.

"I bet you are," I giggled.

Dre squeezed lotion onto my body and rubbed me down. His strong hands massaged every inch of me, and I couldn't do anything but close my eyes and relax. My tense muscles loosened up quickly and became limp.

"That feels so good," I moaned.

Using his elbows, he gave my booty some attention, and I was in heaven. Booty rubs were my favorite. When it came to pleasing me, there was no length he wouldn't take to make me feel appreciated for being me and birthing his child.

It felt like he had been massaging me for hours, and I was in and out of consciousness. But as soon as he straddled me, I was alert because I felt his dick on my ass. Dre pushed my legs apart while I was still on my stomach and climbed in between. The tip of his dick was pressing against my throbbing pussy. Easing his way inside, I gasped a little and raised one of my legs, giving him complete access.

"Mm." Biting down on my lip, I prepared myself for the pleasure I was about to receive. Stroking me slowly, he put his

178

weight on my frame and grabbed my neck with one hand, turning my head toward him. Dre kissed me sloppily on the mouth and bit my neck. He had the softest lips, too.

"This the best pussy I ever had," he said in between breaths. "I might fuck around and get you pregnant again."

The dick was so good I couldn't mumble a word. All I could hear was me moaning and panting constantly. Releasing my neck, he placed both of his arms underneath mine and went so deep in the pussy I thought he hit my bladder.

"Dre!" I moaned.

"It feel good to you, baby?"

"Yes."

I was happy as hell that the baby was in her nursery, because we would've woken her up. Quiet sex was impossible with us, and that's the way I liked it. Siyah just needed to stay asleep until we were done. I wasn't worried about Dre waking up 'cause he would sleep through the night.

His bodyweight had me pinned to the bed, but I still managed to toot my ass up so I could feel every inch going in and out of my slit. "Beat this pussy, baby."

Dre spread my cheeks and put the pound game on my ass. The echoing of skin slapping invaded my ears. Burying my face into the pillow, I screamed into it. He was killin' me.

"Uh-huh, this what you wanted." He gritted his teeth. "Take all yo' dick."

So much time passed that I lost count and it seemed like forever, and with each additional stroke I could feel the soreness arrive, followed by slight pain.

"Sh! Slow down, Dre. I'm sore."

He eased up on me, stroking me slowly before pulling his dick out. I could feel the warmth of his tongue flick across my clit as he ate me from the back. Damn, I loved that shit. Dre sucked on my pussy until I felt myself about to cum.

"Don't stop! I'm about to cum." My knees started to shake, and it wasn't long before I released my juices into his mouth. That was like a breath of fresh air, but that didn't stop him from getting his. Dre slid back in there and fucked me until he got his. Afterward, I cuddled up next to him and kissed his cheek.

"Baby, I've been thinking."

"About what?"

I took a deep breath. "That you should go up and see Tokee tomorrow."

"You sure about that?"

I nodded my head. "Yes, go and see her. I would hate for something to happen to her and you didn't go up there to make sure she was okay. We're the reason she's in there, so go."

"Okay." He rubbed my shoulder, and it wasn't long before we were both knocked out.

***

Dre

When I finally arrived at the hospital, visiting hours were over, but I convinced them to allow me the visit. I told them I was her husband and I just flew into the airport to check on her. As I walked into her room, it was déjà vu all over again. The last time she was here was when she found out she was pregnant with Dre. I told her I didn't want any kids, and she slit her wrists.

Tokee was sound asleep, so I sat down beside her and watched her the way I used to back in the day. We were inseparable when we were younger, and I knew one day I would make her my wife. As time went on and I started making money, I didn't want to be tied down. The lifestyle I lived made me change up the pace. I wanted to party and fuck different chicks, and that was when she got pregnant.

I had just left one of my side chicks when I made it back home to Tokee. She was sitting on the bed with the biggest smile on her face. I took off my jacket and tossed it onto the floor.

"What's up, bae? What you smiling so hard for?"

"I have a surprise for you." She was so excited, and I could hear it in her voice.

"Oh yeah, what's that?"

Tokee got up from the bed and stood in front of me. "Close your eyes and I'll give it to you."

I felt like a little kid at Christmas because I knew this was about to be good, so I squeezed my eyes shut and waited patiently. My dick jumped 'cause I knew I was about to get some head. The coldness of her hands caused me to jump, but I never opened my eyes.

"Give me your hand."

Seconds later I felt an object sitting in the palm of my hand, and when I opened my eyes there was a jewelry box.

"I told you to stop buying me gifts, baby. That's my job to spoil you, not the other way around."

"I know, just open it."

When I opened up the box, the room closed in and I could feel the air being sucked out of it. I was never diagnosed with asthma, but that day it was acting up. Staring at me, bold as the afternoon sun, was a positive pregnancy test. I had to rub my eyes and make sure my eyes wasn't playing tricks on me.

"What the fuck is this?" My hands trembled as everything I clutched in them fell onto the floor.

"We're pregnant, baby." She cupped her hands over her mouth to keep from screaming loudly.

There was only one problem, though: I wasn't happy. I rubbed my hands over my face.

"What's wrong, baby? Aren't you excited?"

"I'm not ready to be a father. There's still so much I wanna do, and a baby was never in the plan."

Tokee's shoulders slouched and her eyes went to the floor. I knew I put a damper on her news. Body language was a muthafucka 'cause I knew how she felt without her saying a word.

"We don't use condoms, so what did you think was gon' happen?"

"Yeah, speaking of which, how the fuck you get pregnant if you on birth control?"

She slid her foot back and forth across the carpet. "I miss a few doses."

All I could do was shake my head 'cause I was pissed off and she knew it. "You probably missed them shits on purpose."

Her head came up slowly, and she looked me in the eyes. "No, I didn't. I just forgot to take them." She paused. "You think I did it on purpose to trap you?"

"I ain't say all that, but you knew I wasn't ready, and this is so convenient right now."

"You know what, Dre, I'm not going through this with you."

Tokee stormed out of the bedroom. I didn't follow her because I was too upset, so I just lay down and dozed off. A few hours later I woke up and she wasn't in the bed, so I got up to look for her. The apartment was only so big, so I quickly found her in the bathroom. I tried to open the door, but she'd locked it, so I knocked.

"Tokee, open the door." There was no answer, so I knocked a few more times. Finally giving up, I went into the kitchen to retrieve a knife. When I made it back to the door, I jimmied the lock and went inside.

Nothing could've prepared me for what I was about to witness.

"Tokee, baby, get up."
Blood was all over the floor, and there was a razor blade lying next to her body. She had slit her wrists. I ran to get my phone and called the paramedics.

Once I snapped back from that nightmare, I decided it was time to wake her up. I rubbed her back gently.

"Tokee, wake up." Her body moved around in the bed. "Come on, get up."

She opened her eyes slightly. "Why you here?"

"I came to check on you."

"Why? It's not like you give a fuck, anyway." She exhaled hard and rolled her eyes. I guess that was her way of letting me know she wasn't happy with my presence. "Who told you I was here, anyway?"

Her attitude was bad, and I was trying my best to ignore it. All I wanted were answers, nothing else, but if she wanted to play nasty I was ready. My mood was foul about the situation anyway 'cause this shit was stupid.

"First of all, kill that attitude. Like this is not what you wanted in the first place. I know what you trying to do, and it ain't gon' work." I sat back and relaxed in the chair.

"Don't get too comfortable. I didn't ask you to come here."

"So, you had your sister call me up here for no reason, huh?" This had her name all over it, but reverse psychology would probably work better on her.

"I don't know what you're talking about. I didn't ask nobody to call you."

"I'm sure this was all a part of your little plan."

"What plan?" she shouted. "If you think I'm trying to trick or trap you, you better think again, because it's not that serious."

"Who are you trying to convince? We both know that's a

lie." My cockiness always got on her nerves, but I knew at any given moment I could have her back. All I had to do was say I was leaving Sierra and she would come running with open arms. "So tell me this: why are you here?"

"It doesn't matter."

"It doesn't matter if you live or die?"

"Nope."

"Did you forget about your Dre?"

"You don't care about him. And besides, he doesn't need me. I'm unstable."

"Are you even listening to yourself? What is wrong with you? If I didn't care about him, he wouldn't be at my house right now."

Tokee sat up in the bed. "You left my baby with that girl?"

"Yep."

"You got to be fuckin' kidding me! I know you didn't just say that."

"What?"

"I don't want him around her!"

"She the reason I'm up here, so fall back. And besides, she ain't gon' do shit to my son."

"She don't have nothing to do with this."

He sat up in the chair. "You wrong about that. She told me I should come and check on you. That girl ain't worried about what you got going on. You the only one that wanna battle."

"Why you always defending that bitch?" she screamed at the top of her lungs.

"You need to calm the fuck down before they call security in here."

"Fuck you and security!" she screamed again.

"That's how you feel?"

"Yes."

"Lyin'-ass."

184

"And what makes you think that?"

I extended my arms out. "Well, this isn't exactly the DoubleTree."

"Go to hell."

"That's exactly where you goin' if you kill yo'self."

"Get the fuck out of my room. I hate you!" She pointed to the door.

"I'm sorry. I shouldn't have said that."

We fell silent for a little while. It was pretty clear things had gotten awkward between us. Shit hasn't been kosher in months.

"Do you still love me?" The tone of her voice changed up completely, and she was back to the soft-spoken woman I knew.

"Huh?"

"Do you still love me?"

"I will always have love for you."

"But you're not in love with me?"

"No."

"So, what do you want me to do? Am I just supposed to turn my feelings off, just like that?"

"Things have changed."

She dropped her head. "So being with her is what you really want?"

"Yes, and I need you to understand that."

"What about me and your son? Do you even care?" She broke down completely. "I can't believe I allowed you to do this to me. I loved you wholeheartedly, and you promised you would never leave me. And all I got was a bunch of broken promises in return."

All this crying was getting on my nerves. We'd been separated for months now, and she was acting like this shit just happened yesterday. It was time to dead this once and for all. I stood up and moved closer to her bed, taking her hands into mine.

"Listen, I'm sorry for all the pain I caused you, but you have to believe me when I say my intention was never to hurt you. I loved you, and all you did was push me away. I wanted to be with you, but you wouldn't keep your uncle out of our business."

"Dre, I'm sorry," she cried, but her tears didn't move me anymore.

"It's a little too late for that, but I will accept your apology. I just want you to know I will be here for you during whatever process you need to go through, but we will never be together again. And I will keep Dre with me, and I will bring him to see you." I let go of her hand. "Get better, Tokee, 'cause Dre needs his mother, and I don't want to keep him away from you."

I walked away so I can get back home to my family.

Chapter 18

Barbee

Monday morning arrived pretty fast, and I was a nervous wreck. I didn't know which way this trial was going to go, but I would find out shortly. Tamela Bryant was standing in front of the courtroom when I arrived.

"Good morning," she said pleasantly.

"Good morning." My mood definitely did not match hers. I was trying to figure out what the fuck she was so happy for. Unless she knew something I didn't know.

I guess she caught my blank stare. "Are you okay?"

"Not really."

"Did you sleep well?"

"Not exactly." What I really wanted to say was *bitch, hell no! First off, my man won't sleep in the same room with me, let alone have sex with me. And on top of that, I'm fighting for my life. So hell no, I'm having a fucked-up day.*

"Okay, well, let's go inside and see what's going on." We walked into the room and took our seats.

Moments later, the bailiff shouted, "All rise," as the judge walked in and took her seat at her bench.

"You may be seated," the judge said. "Mrs. Bryant, are you ready to begin?"

My attorney stood up. "As a matter of fact, I am, judge. I would like to file a motion to dismiss all charges against my client. I have a written statement from Richard Gathers stating he takes all responsibility."

The D.A. stood up and shouted across the room. "Your honor, the defendant, Richard Gathers, has been missing since the transport van blew up on his way to court. How do we know this isn't in their plan to declare a mistrial?"

"This is ridiculous, and it's not my client's fault he's gone MIA. There is no evidence my client murdered the victim, only that she did the clean-up as the defendant recorded her unknowingly. But I ask, where is the video in question? All of a sudden it's gone missing. The witnesses that have come forward also stated my client was, in fact, kidnapped, and that includes the wife of Mr. Gathers. There is no need in drawing out this trial and wasting taxpayers' dollars when the answers are right here in our face."

The judge removed her glasses and sat them beside her. "I have heard all I need to hear, and I have made my decision based on facts and not circumstantial evidence. Ms. Kingston, will you please stand."

A huge lump formed in my throat, and my stomach was in knots. I had no idea where any of this was going. All I knew was I didn't want to go to prison for the rest of my life. Taking slow, steady breaths, I used both hands to pull myself up from the seat. I leaned against the table for support because my legs were weak and felt like noodles. "Yes, your honor?"

"Based on the lack of evidence and the fact the defendant has gone MIA, I am going to dismiss your case. You are free to go home. Case dismissed."

When the judge banged that gavel, I wanted to jump up and down and kiss my attorney on the mouth, but a hug would do her just fine. When I looked behind me, all of my family was there, including Corey. True enough, he was still upset with me, but he rode with me every step of the way, and I was grateful for that. Mercedes blew me a kiss, and I blew her one back. I hadn't seen her in a while, ever since she moved further north, just like she planned. Corey glanced at me for a brief second before he got up and walked out of the courthouse.

***

Corey

Today turned out to be a good day. Barbee was let off scot-free, and I could finally continue with my mission. Everything I set out to do for her was done, and now she could move on with her life. Maybe this would help her focus on her club, since she no longer had to worry about her freedom.

Earlier that morning I spoke with the chief, and he informed me he had already spoken to the judge and everything should go smoothly, but made me promise to call him once it was over to give him an update, so that's what I did. The first time I called his number, it went straight to voicemail, so I called back two more times, but I didn't get an answer. Instead of waiting on his call, I decided to pull up on him at the station, since I knew he would be at work.

When I killed the engine and picked up the keys, my phone slipped in between the seats, so I leaned over in the seat to retrieve them. On my way up, I grabbed the door jam, but I froze. Coming out of the precinct was my father and his wife. This nigga did all that talking about what he wasn't gonna do, and there this bitch-ass nigga was conversing with the enemy. That made my blood boil instantly. The fire in my eyes spit flames in their direction, and I wasn't having that shit. My first thought was to get out and confront them, but I changed my mind. These two would be handled accordingly, and in private.

To ease my mind and make sure I was making the right decision, I hit his phone line to see if he would answer. I watched this man take his phone out of his pocket, look at the screen, and send me to voicemail. That was all I needed to see.

My father stood there watching as she made her way to her car, and once she was on the inside with the engine idling, he went back inside the building. I revved my engine up and pulled out right behind her.

This bitch had me following her all across town to endless and open locations. She headed down Biscayne Boulevard, and I was right in her ass. From the looks of things, she was headed to the Aventura Mall. Keeping myself within a one-car distance, I stayed close until she drove us into the parking garage. My phone started to ring. When I looked down, it was my father.

"Nah, don't call me now. It's too late." I powered the phone off, tossed it into the middle console, and pulled out my gloves to put them on.

The broad took us up to the third floor, and I was cool with that. She whipped into a parking spot, and I did the same. Slipping from the driver's seat, I closed the door quietly. Creeping up to her car, I observed her fixing her hair in the mirror. That was when I jumped into her backseat and closed the door.

"Get out of my car," she screamed.

"Shut the fuck up." I snatched her by the hair and pulled her toward me. "Get a good look at my face, bitch. I want you to know who did this to you."

Her eyes scanned my face, and they grew wider. "You recognize me, huh?"

Her head moved up and down as she whimpered with shallow breaths. "What do you want from me?"

"Every day I ask myself what I could've done to save my mother, and I realize I couldn't do anything to prevent it all because of you. The other day I overheard you and my sperm donor talking about how you set my mom up, and for that I have to get rid of the last piece of the puzzle, just like I did your punk-ass brother." Using my left hand, I unbuckled the belt I was wearing and pulled it from my belt loops. Then I slipped that bitch around her neck, snatching her head back and tightening my grip. She tried to grip it in her hands, but I was too strong for her.

"The more you panic, the longer it will take you to die. So relax and die in peace, 'cause this is really happening."

She clawed at my hands and kicked her feet, but I wasn't letting her go. I watched closely, as her movements grew slower and slower. I had never choked anyone to death, so this was something new. I had to admit it was far cleaner than shooting a muthafucka. There was something about her facial expressions that made me smile.

"You can rest now, Mama. I got this bitch now."

All of her movement finally stopped within minutes, and she was finally dead. My mother's second killer and conspirator had finally taken her last breath.

***

Corey

The chief went all out on the bitch's funeral, and that made me wonder what type of insurance policy he had on that ho. He had her draped in a nice-ass dress, an expensive casket with a horse and carriage. That shit pissed me off, treating that ho like she was a queen or some shit, and we had to struggle to bury my mom while they lived the high life. It was all good, though, 'cause I always handled every situation that came my way.

The repast was at his house, and after all the guest had left we were the last ones there.

"Dre, it's time for us to go. I want to put Siyah to bed."

"A'ight, let's go." Dre stood up and took the baby from Sierra's arms.

"Well, I guess we all leaving together, then. Come on, B."

As soon as I stood up, the chief walked into the room with Ms. Bryant, B's attorney. "Don't leave just yet. I need to talk to y'all."

We all sat back down to listen to what he had to say. And for the attorney to be present, I automatically assumed it was about the closed case against Barbee or some info on the murder of his wife.

"Take a seat, Neil." Tamela placed one hand on his shoulder.

Neil sat down beside Sierra and placed his hand on her knee. She placed hers on his as well, and I could sense she was slowly coming around to him.

"Since Sandra has been killed, I have to renew my will and make sure I take care of the both of you in my passing. I know you felt I didn't take care of you because I wasn't there physically, but financially I did. That doesn't make what I did any better, but I guess it made me feel that way back then. I should've did more as a man and not let her come in between my relationships with my children. My only living children."

He was very emotional as he spoke, but Tamela was right there with him to dry his tears. That made me question their relationship, but that wasn't really my business. As long as that evil wife of his was buried in the dirt, I couldn't care less who he fucked.

"I'm going to sign the will with you right here in the room, and Ms. Bryant here will take care of the rest."

"Thanks, Dad. Everything is going to be okay." Sierra leaned toward him and hugged his neck. The sincerity was definitely there, and I knew she wanted to have that relationship all girls have with their fathers. The relationship Dre shared with Siyah. Even though she was only a baby, he was there for his seed and taking every step to make sure he had a bond with her.

"Thanks, baby."

192

***

Two weeks later, things were back to normal. Or so I thought. When I jumped up out of my sleep, I was drenched in sweat, and the beating from my heart echoed off the walls like a Dr. Dre beat, and I was breathing heavy as hell. This was the third nightmare that week, and they were all about the women in my life and how I failed them as a man by not protecting them. First it was my mother and how I couldn't save her, then Barbee, and last, but certainly not least, the apple of my eye, my baby Sierra.

The room was dark, but I could see Barbee's silhouette underneath the blanket, sleeping so peacefully. There was so much built-up pressure inside of me, and I needed to release it immediately. Removing my boxer briefs, I tossed them onto the floor and eased closer to her warm body. Her ass was tooted in my direction, so I slipped her gown up and smacked my semi-hard dick against it. He stretched out quick, and I slipped him right inside her tight opening and gave it a few pumps. Right away that pussy was wet and she was moaning.

"Sh. Uh."

Slipping my hand underneath her arm, I squeezed her breast and played with her nipples while thrusting my hips forward, giving her added stimulation.

"Shit!" The way her pussy muscle gripped my dick so tight had me about to bust, but I wasn't ready. I had to pull out and shake it in order to stop me from nuttin'.

"Put it back in," Barbee moaned and stuck her ass out farther for me to dig back in those guts.

Flipping her onto her back, I positioned myself between her legs and placed them above my shoulders before sliding back in and sinking deep. "Ooh, this pussy so good," I grunted and started to stroke her.

Flashbacks popped into my head, causing me to dig deeper and deeper. My pace was faster and faster, and her moaning was getting louder by the stroke. I was trying to fuck the air outta her ass. The way her nails dug into my back confirmed the pipe was in her stomach. Sweat was pouring from my head as I beat the brakes off the pussy. My balls slapped hard against her ass.

"Fuck me, baby," she screamed. "I'm about to cum. Beat this pussy up."

The more I pumped, the faster my pace became, and I could feel that build-up creep to the tip of my head. Seconds later, I was depositing every seed into her body.

There was nothing in me that wanted to cuddle, so I got up from the bed and went into the bathroom. I had to piss like a racehorse. Afterward, I flushed the toilet, washed my hands, and cleaned off my dick before I went back into the room to get dressed.

"Where are you going?" Barbee was sitting up on her elbows, watching my every move.

"I'm goin' by Sierra's house to holla at Dre."

"You want me to come?"

"You just did that for me," I couldn't help but laugh.

"That ain't funny."

"I know that, baby, but I'll be right back." I placed a kiss on her forehead and went out the door.

***

Barbee

It was three in the morning when I rolled over to see Corey's side of the bed was empty and cold. I climbed out of bed and stumbled around, looking for him in the dark.

"Corey?" I looked in Sierra's old room, but he wasn't there, so I went into the living room. "Corey?" He was nowhere to be found, so I went back into the room.

"Where the fuck is he?" Mumbling and stomping, I dialed his number and waited for it to start ringing, and as soon as it did I looked around the room. There was chiming coming from by the dresser. When I walked over and pulled out the drawer, Corey's phone was lighting up. Immediately I hung up and called Sierra.

"Hello?" she answered on the third ring.

"I thought I woke you up."

"Nah, I'm up feeding the baby. What's up?"

"Is your bother still there?"

"I haven't seen him."

Her answer made me sit down on the edge of the bed and scratch my head. "He never showed up?"

"No."

"Is Dre home?"

"Not yet, but he should be here soon."

"Okay."

"Is everything okay?"

"Yeah, he left his cellphone at home, and I was trying to see if he was there. I thought him and Dre was together."

"Oh, okay. If he comes here, I'll let him know."

"Goodnight, babes."

"Goodnight."

For the life of me I couldn't understand what the hell was going on and why he left his phone. That was so unlike him. But then it also made me wonder if he left it on purpose. I just hoped he was okay. His safety was more important than anything, and I definitely wasn't worried about no female. Corey would be crazy to cheat on me.

Since there was nothing else left for me to do, I went back to bed and closed these eyes. I was certain he would be home soon.

When I opened up my eyes again several hours later, Corey was snuggled underneath me in a deep sleep. I knew he was tired because he was fully dressed and snoring. My bladder was full, and I needed to relieve myself with the quickness, so I slipped out of bed and went into the bathroom. The toilet seat was cold as hell when I sat down. I was so tired I couldn't wait to get back in bed and snuggle up with my honey. The way he fucked me last night snatched all my energy, and I needed to rejuvenate.

After I was done, I flushed the toilet and washed my hands and high-tailed it back to the bed. I was curious to see what time it was, and I probably needed to text Sierra and let her know he made it home in one piece. Picking up my phone, I clicked the button to light up the screen and saw I had eleven missed calls from Sierra. I dialed her number a few times, but she didn't answer.

Now I was panicking, so I shook Corey from his sleep. "Wake up. Wake up." He didn't move, so I shook him again. "Babe, get up."

"Yeah." The sound of his voice was groggy.

"Get up! We have to check on your sister."

He finally opened his eyes. "What's wrong with her?"

"I don't know, but I have eleven missed calls from her and she's not picking up the phone."

"Okay, okay." It took a few more minutes to get him up, but once he got out of bed we were able to bust a move.

On our way there I kept calling her phone, but she still wasn't answering, and that made me feel a little uneasy. I knew Dre wasn't home when I called that morning, which made matters worse knowing she was alone the last time we spoke.

Any other day it only took us a good fifteen minutes to get

196

to their house, but all of a sudden since there was an emergency, here came all this traffic out of nowhere. I was so antsy.

"Did you see Dre last night?"

"Nah." Corey kept his eyes on the road at all times. Not once did he look in my direction.

"I thought that's where you went." I was trying to question him without making it sound like an interrogation.

"I was headed there, but then something came up and I needed to go handle it."

"That's why you left your phone?"

"Just ask me the real question: if I was with a bitch last night."

"I ain't worried about that."

"You worried about something."

This nigga was pissing me off just that fast, so I shifted my body toward the passenger window and folded my arms. "Not at all."

I could see him looking at me from the corner of my eye, but I didn't bother to say a word. I just sat back in silence, waiting for the last two minutes in the car to be over. We were finally inside the neighborhood.

When we pulled into the driveway, Dre's car wasn't there, but Sierra's truck was. That's when I jumped out of the car and did a beeline for the front door. Corey was right in my ass like some brake lights. To my surprise, it was open, and nothing could've prepared us for the sight that we were about to see. Sierra was sitting on the floor with Siyah clutched in her arms tightly, rocking back and forth with a face full of tears. In my heart I knew something was wrong, and I knew it had to be Dre. We both rushed to be by her side. Corey took the baby.

"What's wrong?"

"He's dead," she cried.

"Who's dead? Is it Dre?"

She pointed at the television screen, and I could not believe my eyes. My heart began to race because my greatest fear had been confirmed, and I felt so bad for her because this was a pain I never wanted her to endure. All I could do was hold her in my arms and console her.

When I looked over at Corey, he was rocking the baby in his arms in silence, looking at the news as well. His face held no emotion whatsoever.

Chapter 19

Corey

Seeing my sister in such pain was doing a number on my heart, but I didn't think she would be so affected. At this point it didn't matter, though, because it was too late and there was no such thing as turning back the hands of time. As I watched Barbee's actions toward her, I thought back to what happened.

The nightmares had me thinking, and I knew I needed to do one last thing before I lost my mind completely. All I could do was think about my mother and shed tears. Standing at the front door with an oversized coat on, my face was moist from crying as I knocked on the door. I could hear the locks being removed before the door swung open.

"Hey, son. What's wrong?"

"I need to talk to you."

My father took a step back and extended his arm. "Come in. I have all the time in the world."

I walked in and we went into the living room and sat down on the sofa. He was on one side, and I was on the other.

"What's on your mind?"

"My mother," I said flatly, and I could see the discomfort in his eyes. That was a subject I was sure he didn't want to speak on.

"What about her?"

"What happened to her?" I wiped my eyes with my hand. "I know what the news said, but I need to know what really happened to her and why she isn't here with her kids and grandchild."

That alone should've told him I knew something and to not bullshit me. He was silent for a few seconds before he finally spoke up.

"Son, all I can tell you is she was murdered by her boyfriend, but you know that already. You caught up with him and shot him, remember?"

"Oh yeah, I remember what I did, and he deserved it." I scooted to the edge of the seat. "But what I'm trying to get at is why was I released from the system like that so early? I know you had something to do with that, of course. All my life I've been in trouble, but yet I still have no record. There is nothing in the system that states anything. Not even a simple ticket."

My father's shoulders were quite tense, and I sensed there was something he wanted to say, but he couldn't find the words to say it. Or he didn't want to.

"Corey, I may not have been in your life physically, but I made sure you had a clear shot at any and everything you could've possibly wanted to do in life. Every time I looked you up and you had been arrested, I made sure I took care of that because you wouldn't get far in life as a black man with strikes against him. I did all I could do up until now, and I want to make things right between us."

"And why would you want to make things right between us?"

A sudden crease appeared in his brow. "Because y'all are my kids, and I should've been there from day one instead of allowing other things to get in between that."

"Oh, you mean your wife?" I rubbed my hands together. "You sure that ain't the guilt from your actions that's making you wanna do right?"

"Guilt?" he frowned. "What guilt? I haven't done anything."

I nodded my head. "Oh yeah, you've done plenty."

"All I'm guilty of is not being there the way a father is supposed to be, and that's it."

This nigga was getting on my nerves with all the lying, and I couldn't take it no more. I reached inside my coat and pulled out my best bitch, who loved to clap for a nigga. "Let's stop fuckin' around and get to the facts."

"Corey, put the gun away."

I bit down on my bottom lip. "Not until you come clean about what you did."

"I didn't do anything."

"You lying, and don't make me have to use this on you."

"I swear I didn't do anything."

Out of frustration, I kicked the coffee table that sat in between us. "See, you about to piss me off, 'cause I hate a liar." I rose to my feet. "Let me just fill you in on a little something I know. The facts. See, I know my mother's death was a well thought-out plan by that bitch you loved and cared for more than your own kids."

The moment his eyes grew wide, I knew I had him by the balls.

"You allowed her to walk free for years knowing what she did to my mom, and I'll never forgive you for that. Her brother shot and killed my mom in cold blood. Do you know how that feels, to see the one you love die in front of you? To choke on her own blood and take her last breath?"

"Me turning her in wasn't gon' bring her back, and in return you killed her brother."

"That's because you wasn't man enough to handle it. I had to do it. A part of me died inside when I lost her. She was the only person in the world who loved me and my sister."

"That's not true. I love the both of you."

"Bullshit."

"It's true."

"I want to let you in on a little secret, though." I paused where I stood so I could get a good look at his face. "I killed

Sandra. I took that bitch out for what she did to my mother."

"What?"

"You heard me. I killed that bitch. That day we were here having dinner and she walked in here mad, I overheard the conversation between y'all, and she said she left her diary out for you to see. And when you saw it, you never confronted her about it, so that made you just as guilty."

The chief grabbed his chest and took a few breaths. "You. You killed her."

My sinister laugh filled the room. "Of course I did. I choked that bitch to death with my belt at the Aventura Mall. And she deserved it, too. But this the funny thing: you argued with her and told her she would no longer keep you away from your kids. Then I roll up on you at your job and she's there, talking to you. That was betrayal at its finest for me."

"Corey, this is all a big misunderstanding."

"Nah, everything is clear to me, and I'm about to send you to be with your wife."

"Corey, please."

He held his hands up, begging for his life. I wasn't fazed one bit. Raising the gun, I pointed it at his head and paused for a second. "I'll do you one better. You kill yo'self and end all of this."

"Son, you don't want me to do that." Sweat dripped from his forehead.

"Nigga, don't call me son! For me to be a son, you would have to be a father, and muthafucka, you don't deserve that title. That's flat out disrespectful." I pulled out a second gun and walked over to where he sat. "Take this gun and blow your brains out. If you do anything other than what I'm telling you, I'll pull the trigger myself." I handed him my other bitch. "Put this in your mouth and pull the fuckin' trigger."

His hands trembled while I pressed the heat to his temple.

Finally taking the gun, he placed it in his mouth, and I could see the hesitation.

"Now pull the trigger," I demanded.

The chief closed his eyes and fired the shot. The back of his head exploded, sending brain matter all over the place.

Siyah's crying got my attention and shook me from my thoughts. Barbee was finally able to get Sierra to stop crying and into bed. She knew that bitch-ass nigga for all of ten minutes and she was so hurt by his death. I guess a father and daughter bond was important to her, 'cause it didn't mean shit to me.

The sound of the front door closing let me know Dre had finally made it in. When he walked into the room, he went straight to Sierra.

"Baby, I'm here. Everything is going to be okay."

He took her into his arms and embraced her. "Thanks for coming to check on my baby. I had a little business to handle early this morning."

"You know we got her, bruh," Barbee answered him and then walked over to me, smiling. "You look like you ready for one of your own."

"I might be."

She grabbed my head and pulled me close to her. "This has your name all over it. You don't have to say anything now, but I know it, and that's why you left your phone home."

I couldn't say shit 'cause her muthafuckin' ass knew me like a book.

Destiny Skai

Epilogue

Barbee

Ten months later

It was Siyah's first birthday, and we were celebrating with a party at the park. I had to admit Dre and Sierra went all out for their baby girl. She was too cute, dressed in her pink, lace tutu with some bedazzled pink Chuck Taylors. The princess theme was perfect for her because that's exactly what she was. The DJ was playing kiddie music, and the children were bouncing around everywhere.

Over the past several months I had to admit things had really taken a turn for the best, and I couldn't be happier. Corey finally decided to let go of the past and move forward by setting a date for our wedding. We did so much making up and catching up for lost time that in the midst of it all, a blessing came our way. In the next few weeks I would be giving birth to our baby boy. Of course, when I found out I was happy, but I was filled with so much anxiety all because of the tragic way I lost the first child. But Corey had been there every step of the way, making sure I was good.

"Hey, Barbee, you looking good. You're just glowing." Tokee sat down beside me, clutching her purse.

"Thank you. Why you just getting here? Black folks always late," I laughed.

"Girl, my slow-ass client was late."

"Oh, okay."

"Where is my baby? I don't see him." Tokee looked around to scan the area. "Oh, yes, I do. I'll be right back." She got up and walked away with her purse tightly in hand. Looking in the direction she was walking I could see she was heading to where

Sierra was standing with Dre.

Tokee had finally realized the fact she and Dre were over and she needed to move on with her life. They were able to co-parent without a problem, and all the drama had finally stopped. After she was released from the hospital, she took some counseling to help her get over him, so that was the first step. Now she was doing better.

My fat ass got tired of sitting down, so I got up and went to where Sierra was standing.

"Hey, twin." She rubbed my belly and smiled. "I can't wait to meet my nephew."

"Girl, me either. I'm tired of him sitting on my damn bladder."

"Shit, how you think I feel? I have to carry around this big-ass stomach and chase Siyah around the house. I told Dre this is it for us. He must think I'm a baby-making machine. Two kids by the time I hit 18 is a lot."

"I hear that, but at least you with the daddy, and you taking college courses right now, so you good. Fuck what everybody else say."

"Yeah, I know, but still that's a lot of responsibility."

"Well, you better get on birth control and stop putting it on that man like that."

"Now you sound like him. He be like, 'bae, I can't pull out 'cause it's so good.'" To hear her imitate his voice was funny. We both cracked up in laughter.

"Can I have your attention, please?" When we both turned around, it was the DJ making an announcement. "Sierra, come to the front, please. I need to ask you a question."

Both of us walked up to the booth where Dre was standing next to Corey, smiling conspiratorially.

"What's going on?" asked Sierra.

Dre took the mic from the DJ, and then he turned to my girl

and looked her in the eyes. "Baby, I want you to know you're the best thing that ever happened to me, and I can't imagine life without you. You gave me my first daughter, and now we have another baby on the way. I love the way you care for my son even though he doesn't belong to you. For that, and for a whole lot of other reasons, I owe you the world and a happiness that will last forever." He slowly went down to one knee, looking up at Sierra lovingly.

Sierra instantly started to hyperventilate. She was fanning herself and wiping her tears before he could utter a single word. Overwhelmed with emotion, she placed her hand on her belly and rocked side to side like she was about to go into labor. This lasted for about a minute before she finally stopped and looked down into his eyes.

In a deep and strong voice laced with pure love, he said the words that made her face light up. "Sierra, baby, will you marry me?"

Out of nowhere she started jumping up and down like she wasn't strapped with that big-ass baby in tow. If I hadn't known any better, I would've thought the bitch had to pee.

I started giggling at her happiness. The moment was so beautiful and touching, and Sierra deserved it.

Dre had the biggest smile on his face while watching her bounce around in excitement. Even with all of her movement, he never let go of her hand.

"I can't believe this is happening." Her voice was raspy, but thanks to the microphone we heard her just fine.

"So, what's your answer?" he chuckled.

"Yes. Yes! Of course I'll marry you." The response rushed out of her mouth.

Dre slipped the ring onto her finger, and then he stood up and kissed her deeply. She hugged him tightly and got all into the kiss.

Out of the corner of my eye, I saw Tokee walk over and sit down at the table where I had been sitting. I wondered what was on her mind. Dre was a helluva nigga to lose. Would she truly accept it and keep it moving? Or would this finally push her over the edge?

Bitch better stay in her lane.

After the proposal, I went back to my seat across from Tokee. I didn't feel too well.

It seemed like she was in a daze. "He seems so happy." She didn't blink once.

"Yeah, he is. But don't you worry, you will find your happiness, as well," I comforted.

"Yeah, I know. I'm in a good place right now."

Her eyes shifted up, so I looked to see what she was looking at, and standing there was Sierra with a huge smile on her face. "Congratulations on your engagement," she offered.

Sierra nodded her head. "Thank you."

Tokee stood up. "I also want to congratulate you on the baby."

"Thank you. I appreciate that," Sierra replied sweetly.

"I also want to thank you for caring for my son and taking my husband away from me." Sarcasm dripped from her words like thick blood spilling from the end of a sharp knife.

"What?" Sierra placed her hands on her belly.

"You can't possibly think you can build happiness using my foundation of hurt to build a home." Her face twisted up. Just that quickly, her happy place seemed to dissipate.

As soon as she said that, I stood up to address her. "You need to g'on 'head with all that. If you still salty, then maybe you should leave."

"Okay, I'll do that. But before I go, let me give you the baby's gift."

Tokee reached inside her purse, and when she pulled her

208

hand out, she was holding a small handgun close to Sierra's stomach. Her hand trembled as she tried to keep it steady. "Bitch, you ruined my life. And if I can't have him, you can't, either."

Before I could react, she fired two shots.

Pow! Pow!

Everyone in attendance screamed and took cover behind tables and chairs. Sierra's body dropped to the ground and Tokee took off running toward the parking lot.

"Dre!" I screamed. My first instinct was to go to her aid, but I couldn't move. It was like I was stuck in cement.

He and Corey came running, and as soon as he saw Sierra's body on the ground, he lost it. "Baby, what happened?" he cried as he got down on the ground next to her and cradled her head in his arms. "Wake up, baby, please. Please don't go." Dre was shaking her and moving her head around. I could see her eyes fluttering, as tears streamed down her face.

"It hurts, Dre," she moaned pitifully.

"I know, baby. Just hold on for me, please," he begged. "Help will be here soon. Just don't close your eyes."

"Somebody call the police," I screamed.

Corey grabbed me by my shoulders and shook me. "B, what happened?"

"Tokee shot her," I cried.

"I'ma kill that bitch," he spat and took off running in her direction.

This was too much to bear. I sank to the ground and tearfully watched Dre scream and cry as he watched the love of his life fade away. Seeing death up close and personal was like second nature to me, but this hurt. It hurt like hell.

I cried for Sierra, and I cried for myself because I was supposed to be dead a long time ago. The life I lived was so dangerous, and I was still here. All she did was fall in love, and now she was fighting for her life. Clutching my belly, I rocked back and forth and screamed to the top of my lungs in pure agony.

When my loud cry simmered to low whimpering, I heard Sierra whisper, "Dre, I'm so cold." Her bottom lip quivered.

"I'll keep you warm, baby. Just promise me you won't leave me." He removed his shirt and placed it over her arms and held her close to his chest.

"I'm dying, Dre, but I'll love you until my last breath," she said faintly.

He kissed her lips. "No, Sierra, you're gonna be okay. Fight that shit, baby. For us! I love you more than life itself, and I'm nothing without you. Sierra, please don't go. I can't live without you."

Sierra's eyes fluttered, then rolled to the top of her head. Her chest rose and fell for the last time.

She was gone.

Dre placed his hand over her eyes and closed them as streams of tears ran down his face. "She's gone. My baby is gone."

"Oh God! Why?" I screamed.

Dre looked down into Sierra's face; it was clear the life had drained out of her. He pressed his lips to hers and kissed her tenderly. "Baby, don't you worry. I'm gon' kill that bitch. I promise you that." He looked up at me with the nastiest scowl on his face. "She killed my baby. She gon' pay for that!"

I sniffled. "Handle ya' business, bruh. You know what needs to be done."

I took one last look at Sierra. Never in a million years did I think this would be the outcome of our story. To see her on the ground, murdered in cold blood, was just as painful as seeing Chyna die in front of me. My heart ached tremendously. I couldn't stop the tears falling from my eyes.

210

When the paramedics arrived a short time later and loaded Sierra into the truck, we all knew there was nothing they could do to reverse death. It was forever, as was our pain.

As the ambulance raced from the scene, I prayed that at least they would save the baby she was carrying.

***

A week later, Sierra was laid to rest. The doctor was able to save the baby through an emergency C-section. It was a blessing the bullet missed him. There was no way we could handle two deaths at once. Dre was grateful for his son, but losing Sierra was really hard for him. He spent a majority of his time at our house because he couldn't pull himself to sleep in the home he shared with the love of his life. At this point he was a single dad and was forced to raise his kids without their mother, but with help from Corey, Mercedes, and I, he would be just fine.

After the murder, Mercedes made her way back down to Broward County to spend more time with us since she went missing after her kidnapping. That was what she needed in order to get over everything bad that happened in our lives.

Slipping on my house shoes, I went outside to check the mailbox. As I walked through the hallway, I felt a cold chill come over me, causing me to shiver. I knew I needed to hurry up and get back inside. Sticking the key in the slot, I unlocked the box and pulled out tons of junk mail. I tossed the unnecessary shit in the trash and kept what was important. One of the letters slipped from my hands, and I bent down to pick it up. The newspaper on the ground caught my attention, so I grabbed it and took it out of the plastic.

The front page read, *"Woman's Body Found Decapitated."* As I continued to read, my heart rate increased when I stumbled upon a familiar name: Tokee Williams. I heaved a sigh of relief because it was finally over. Just the thought of my sisters made my tears flow heavily like a running faucet. I walked to the end of the hallway and looked up at the sky. The sun was shining so brightly, and I knew all my bitches were smiling down on me.

I raised my fist up in the air and grinned. "He got that bitch, sis, just like he said he would. I'm talkin' 'bout he took that ho's head off her shoulders. You don't know how that shit got me feeling right now. But rest on, baby girl. I promise to take care of those babies for you. Dre, too." I could feel myself choking up, so I paused to catch my breath. Placing my hand on my chest, I took a few quick breaths and yelled.

"She took you from your kids, and that shit hurt 'cause Siyah looks for you every day, but I got her. I won't let you down, sis. I love you, and I'll keep your memory alive until we meet again."

My experiences had been a brutal teacher, but they molded me into the woman I had become. Deep in my heart I would always be a Fetti Girl, but the time had come for me to put that life behind me forever. I lost so many people I loved, and I would never get them back. All I had were precious memories that would never fade away.

Corey Jr. was set to enter this world in two more weeks, and I needed to be there to raise my child. Once the dust settled, Operation Chyna Dolls would be back up and running, and I would be bigger and better than I was before.

Before I walked off, I blew a kiss to the sky. "Rest in peace, Fetti Girls."

The End

Stay Connected with Us!

Text **LOCKDOWN** to 22828 to stay up-to-date with new releases, sneak peaks, contests and more…

Thank you!

Destiny Skai

Coming Soon from Lock Down Publications/Ca$h Presents

BOW DOWN TO MY GANGSTA

By **Ca$h & Jamaica**

TORN BETWEEN TWO

By **Coffee**

BLOOD OF A BOSS **IV**

By **Askari**

BRIDE OF A HUSTLA **III**

By **Destiny Skai**

WHEN A GOOD GIRL GOES BAD **II**

By **Adrienne**

LOVE & CHASIN' PAPER **II**

By **Qay Crockett**

THE HEART OF A GANGSTA **II**

By **Jerry Jackson**

LOYAL TO THE GAME **IV**

By **T.J. & Jelissa**

A DOPEBOY'S PRAYER **II**

By **Eddie "Wolf" Lee**

TRUE SAVAGE **III**

By **Chris Green**

IF LOVING YOU IS WRONG… **II**

214

By **Jelissa**
BLOODY COMMAS **II**
By **T.J. Edwards**
A DISTINGUISHED THUG STOLE MY HEART **II**
By **Meesha**
ADDICTIED TO THE DRAMA **II**
By **Jamila Mathis**

Available Now
(CLICK TO PURCHASE)
RESTRAINING ORDER **I & II**
By **CA$H & Coffee**
LOVE KNOWS NO BOUNDARIES **I II & III**
By **Coffee**
RAISED AS A GOON I, II & III
By **Ghost**
LAY IT DOWN **I & II**
LAST OF A DYING BREED
By **Jamaica**
LOYAL TO THE GAME
LOYAL TO THE GAME II
LOYAL TO THE GAME III

By **TJ & Jelissa**

BLOODY COMMAS

By **T.J. Edwards**

IF LOVING HIM IS WRONG…

By **Jelissa**

A DISTINGUISHED THUG STOLE MY HEART

By **Meesha**

PUSH IT TO THE LIMIT

By **Bre' Hayes**

BLOOD OF A BOSS **I II & III**

By **Askari**

THE STREETS BLEED MURDER **I, II & III**

THE HEART OF A GANGSTA

By **Jerry Jackson**

CUM FOR ME

CUM FOR ME 2

CUM FOR ME 3

An **LDP Erotica Collaboration**

BRIDE OF A HUSTLA **I & II**

THE FETTI GIRLS **I & II**

By **Destiny Skai**

WHEN A GOOD GIRL GOES BAD

By **Adrienne**

A GANGSTER'S REVENGE **I II III & IV**

THE BOSS MAN'S DAUGHTERS

THE BOSS MAN'S DAUGHTERS II

A SAVAGE LOVE **I & II**

BAE BELONGS TO ME

A HUSTLER'S DECEIT I, II

By **Aryanna**

A KINGPIN'S AMBITON

A KINGPIN'S AMBITION **II**

I MURDER FOR THE DOUGH

By **Ambitious**

TRUE SAVAGE

TRUE SAVAGE II

By **Chris Green**

A DOPEBOY'S PRAYER

By **Eddie "Wolf" Lee**

WHAT ABOUT US **I & II**

NEVER LOVE AGAIN

THUG ADDICTION

By **Kim Kaye**

THE KING CARTEL **I, II & III**

By **Frank Gresham**

Destiny Skai

THESE NIGGAS AIN'T LOYAL **I, II & III**

By **Nikki Tee**

GANGSTA SHYT **I II &III**

By **CATO**

THE ULTIMATE BETRAYAL

By **Phoenix**

BOSS'N UP **I & II**

By **Royal Nicole**

I LOVE YOU TO DEATH

By Destiny J

I RIDE FOR MY HITTA

I STILL RIDE FOR MY HITTA

By **Misty Holt**

LOVE & CHASIN' PAPER

By **Qay Crockett**

TO DIE IN VAIN

By **ASAD**

218

BOOKS BY LDP'S CEO, CA$H

(CLICK TO PURCHASE)

TRUST IN NO MAN

TRUST IN NO MAN 2

TRUST IN NO MAN 3

BONDED BY BLOOD

SHORTY GOT A THUG

THUGS CRY

THUGS CRY 2

THUGS CRY 3

TRUST NO BITCH

TRUST NO BITCH 2

TRUST NO BITCH 3

TIL MY CASKET DROPS

RESTRAINING ORDER

RESTRAINING ORDER 2

IN LOVE WITH A CONVICT

Coming Soon

BONDED BY BLOOD 2

BOW DOWN TO MY GANGSTA

Destiny Skai